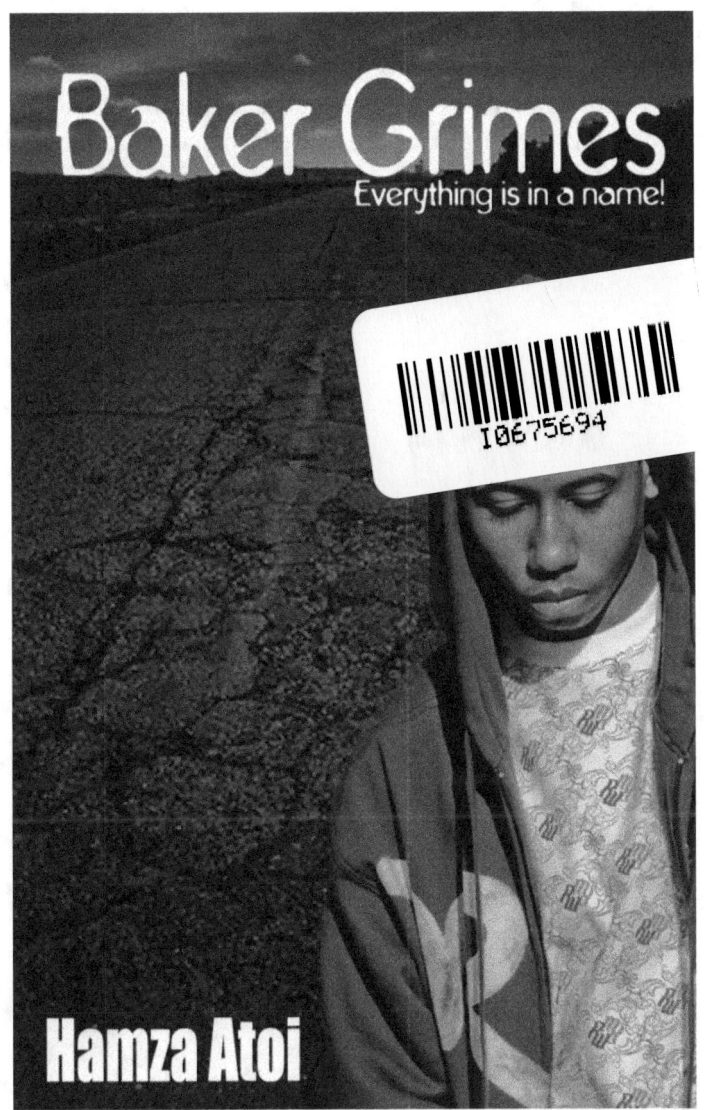

This novel is a work of fiction. Any resemblances to actual events, real people, living or dead, organizations, establishments, and locales are products of the author's imagination. Other names, characters, places, and incidents are used fictitiously.

Published By HA Publishing, LLC
Baker Grimes
Copyright © 2011 by Hamza Atoi

Library of Congress Catalog Number: TXu 1-800-037
ISBN Number: 978-0615618487

Cover Design/Photography: Hamza Atoi
Cover Model: Marcus Jai Evans

For my family...Park Place/Colonial Place included.
-Hamza Atoi

In loving memory of those who left all too sudden

Donell Stepney
Darryl "Divine" Nix
Terrance "Pork" Parker
Will "Da real One" Bell
Bernard "35th Street" Brown
Eric Skinner
Major Clark
Breon "Bucks" Ethridge
Powerhouse
Mango
Shampoo
Lil Eric
Big Eric
Cedric Cochran
Kevin McClammy
Brian McClammy
Lil David
Michael Corprew
Pimp
Anwar Dixon
Reggie "La Red" Davis
Ricky Nellum
Thomas Barnes
Thomas Holmes
Antwaun & Desmond
Piggy
Lil Ralph
Boonie
Wayne Moore
Pernell Taylor
Sunny
Lil Willie aka Pete the dog
Colonial Place Red
Marcus Upshur
Coolie
Milton Thomas

"Hamza Atoi's book: "Baker Grimes" will be highly embraced within the literary canon of street literature. The level of storytelling in his novel is way beyond most books in its genre. He was able to make each character have his/her own personality without bleeding into other characters which is a skill not easy to acquire. I was riveted from the start, as I was taken from reader to bystander to participant. This book will indeed embrace the mantle of the likes of Donald Goines and others of his caliber. Salute!"
-Bruce George, Co-Founder of Russell Simmons, Def Poetry Jam on HBO

"Hamza Atoi has the promise of being one of the best authors of this generation. His writing style possesses the same engaging, raw, thought-provoking honesty that is reminiscent of the legendary literary great Richard Wright and the critically acclaimed Nathan McCall. Whether it's in a novel or in his poetic prose, Atoi's artistry will grab and mesmerize you from the first word to the last."

-- Angel Baker from OnTheVerge.com and author of the book "The Last Writes".

Baker Grimes
Hamza Atoi
CHAPTER ONE

They say everything is in a name. Your name is part of the path destiny holds for you and I believe it because my name seems like it chose the direction my life would take once I was born.

My name is Baker Grimes. I am my mother's only child. She gave birth to me in the midst of a drug raid that took place at our small apartment in Park Place. The story goes like this. Mama Maria was part of a Dominican drug ring that stretched from Norfolk Virginia to Brooklyn New York. She started her career out as one of the enforcers for the crew she was in. Murder by seduction was how she moved. Her beautiful bronze skin, long black hair, 5'11 140 pound frame with a face like the sound of God's voice spelled disaster for those who were clueless of her capabilities. Her walk was elegant, and luring. Men marveled at her finessed features, and that's what made her DANGEROUS!

I don't know much about my father. He was a loving and caring man from what my mother says. He was an ordinary workingman, not a hustler. He died from cancer a month before I was born. I do know this; Mother Maria loved him dearly because each time he was spoken of she'd go into the room and cry. That showed and proved her love because she never cried about anything.

My mother received 20 years for a murder when I was 7 years old, so the majority of my life I lived with my grandmother Rosa. She was a beautiful and spiritual woman. She loved Jesus and made no apologies about it. She dragged us to church on Sundays and never allowed us to make an excuse about why we didn't want to go. That is what makes this story a little more interesting. I know God and understand His foundation and principles. I just...we'll...let me get to the rest of the story without spoiling it.

My grandfather died when I was two years old and left my grandmother with a large sum of insurance money. She would tithe faithfully, always giving God the first fruits of her harvest. I saw how He truly blessed her with financial freedom and I also saw the day the devil stepped in to offer what only God could give.

My grandmother and I lived in the Colonial Place section of Norfolk. It is a small suburb not a stone's throw away from the notorious streets of Park Place. My mother's twin sister and her son Sammy lived about five minutes away from us. I was eleven and Sammy was thirteen years old when the lifestyle we grew accustomed to begin.

Sammy knew the streets. He grew up on 35th and Debree. When we were younger I spent a lot of time at Sammy and Aunt Marisa's house. My Aunt was the type of aunt that would give you the shirt off her back but she was raw an uncut. She stood about the same height as my mom but a little more on the hefty side. She was the one who would bang girls up in school if they stepped out of line. She had hands out of this world. She even knocked dudes out back then. She would curse you out without hesitation. Let her tell it, we were always tearing up things, so most of our time was spent outside. We weren't bad kids, but we definitely stayed in the middle of trouble. Its funny how the devil operates because one would think if you had a praying family member everyone in that family would be Holy. That is far from true. The only one who wore the banner of righteousness in our family was granny. Everyone else was stone cold sinners.

Down the street from Sammy's house was a small convenient store called, "Red Ball." We hung out there and in front of *Kings* (*The king of Snowball*) on 35th street the majority of the time with our little crew. It was Sammy, Clarkboy, Hawk, Swampman, Tony Small, and I. Everyone respected us because of my mom and aunt. The old heads on the block would always tell us that one day our crew would take over Park Place. We weren't thinking about that because all we wanted to do was boost candy from Red Ball, and play *hide and go get* with the neighborhood girls.

My Aunt Marisa could care less about what we did. Most of the time she wanted us out of her face, so she paid us to stay outside. She had this big time boyfriend Mr. Maurice. We loved Mr. Maurice because he always came bearing gifts. I remember when Atari first came out. I was one of the first kids to get it. Mr. Maurice told us, "I got something better than Atari," and gave Sammy a *Coleco Vision* game. It was a dope video game and two times better than Atari. At Sammy's house we had two TV's in his room, one for my Atari, and one for the Coleco Vision. When Aunt Marisa wasn't home we used the games to get paid. We charged a quarter just to get in the house, another quarter for two games of Combat which was on my Atari, and fifty-cents for the Coleco Vision game. By the end of the day we had $10 dollars between the two of us. Our boys were able to play for free. They also acted as our marketing reps because after they would leave, they would go back to the streets and tell the kids how sweet our games were. They got their hustle on too. They would tell the neighborhood kids the only way to get to the door was to pay them a quarter also. We all got paid. Everyone was happy. Sammy and I never stressed over money because between Grandma, Mr. Maurice, and our hustle we always had it, but Sammy said he knew a way that we could get more.

There was this old head we knew named "Big Sippi." Big Sippi was this heroin hustler from Mississippi, and one of the ones who came over Auntie's house playing spades. He was the one that told us our crew would hold Park Place down one day, and always pulled Sam to the side to try to convince us to be lookout boys.

Big Sippi wasn't to be trusted though. It was said once he was the reason my mom caught her murder charge. Nobody really knew if it was true, but I knew he had something with him. It was all in his eyes. Even at my young age, he couldn't look me in my face. He would always smirk and look away. I never did like him, but for Sammy, I was ride or die. If Sammy wanted to be down with his crew, I was going to be down with his crew. We were always in front of Red ball playing anyway, so I figured what the hell! It was like making free money for doing what you normally do on a daily basis

Late that night, we convinced Aunt Marisa to let Swampman, Tony, Clarkboy, and Hawk spend the night with us. We sat up all night playing video games and discussing what to do about Big Sippi's offer to be on his team as lookouts. It didn't take long before all of us agreed. The next day we met up with Big Sippi to converse about the payment.

"Y'all little dudes made the right choice to mess with me and ya'll gone make mo' money than dat' game hustle ya'll were pushing."

He said he was going to pay us as a crew. We had one set price for six hours a day. The only catch was we all had to work, and the price for our labor would be 300 dollars a week. We all looked at each other like kids about to win the candy lotto. Sammy and I had seen money like that, but for us to be able to handle all that money made things easy, but I didn't let the money go to my head. I still didn't trust that hillbilly, and as far as I was concerned, he was going to be watched.

The summer had come and school was out. It was time for us to do our thing. Swampman, Tony, and I posted up in front of the Red ball. We were in a triangular setting. Sammy, Clarkboy, and Hawk were the front set of eyes in front of the store so they could see everything coming down the 35th side. Swampman Tony and I roamed, throwing the ball so we could see all other angles. We didn't miss anything. We had a special whistle for the cops and another for suspected undercover cops and snitches. We knew the whole blueprint of how cops would set things up. We watched out for U-Haul trucks or any moving vans because the "Jump outs" (tactical narcotics team) loved to use inconspicuous vehicles. We knew faces and watched for anything that looked out of place from the normal traffic moving through Park Place. What made us undetectable was the fact we were kids, and it was normal to cops to see kids playing outside of the store. I must admit; Big Sippi did know what he was doing. He wasn't a dumb guy, I'll give him that much.

Previously, before we took post on the block, Big Sippi had some older heads posted up. He saw us playing outside every day, hustling video games, and put the family history of Sammy and I together. Man, hell…it didn't take a rocket scientist, or someone with a bachelor's degree to know we were money. He also saved money with making the move with us. His payroll went down because by us being kids, $300 between all of us for the week was a jackpot. He was paying his other team $150 dollars a day. Big Sippi was a smart dude all right. He didn't cut them off. He just gave them more responsibility for the same pay. We also never had a problem from Aunt Marisa. As long as we were out of her hair, we were good. I often wondered why she never caught on, but at the time, I didn't care. She never said anything, so we kept it moving.

Grandma Rosa on the other hand was always suspicious. I stopped asking for money, but it wasn't hard to get her off our trail because of Mr. Maurice. I told her Mr. Maurice paid us fifty dollars a week if we kept the house clean. After that she never gave me any hassle. She had no reason not to trust me.

We joined Big Sippi's crew in the summer of 1985. That is when I can actually say it stared for us. We never knew what life had in store and we really didn't care at that point. Life's complications didn't introduce itself to kids and neither did we want to meet her. Having fun was all that matter for our crew and making money doing what we love to do was more fun than we could have ever imagined.

Sam, Hawk, and Clarkboy were headed to the 8th grade, and Tony, Swampman, and I were headed to the 6th grade. The crazy thing was, now Blair Junior High was Blair Middle School and they were taking 6th graders too. We were all at school together! It made the crew solid! We all couldn't wait for the first day of school because we all were going to have money and clothes. For Sammy and I, we always had gear, so that wasn't anything special to us. It just felt good that the whole crew had gear together. We all were fresh to death. Big Sippi told us when the school year begun, he was going to cut our hours back. He never finished school, so to him school was important. He said that he had also set up tutors for us if we needed them. He was going to make sure we were taking care of. We were his moneybags, and he was beginning to be all right with me.

One day, I was sitting on the porch at Grandma Rosa's; Big Sippi drove past, saw me on the porch, backed up, and parked. He got out of a Candy apple red Deuce & a Quarter dressed in a Suit and Gator boots. His hands looked like he had Fort Knox on his knuckles. His whole front grill was full of gold teeth that shined like the sun. He looked and smelled like money. He walked on the porch and sat down beside me,

"What's up little NGHA? Why you sitting here like you lost your crew?"

"I'm just cooling." I said with a mellow tone.

"Your boys are down at your auntie's, so why you here?"

I told him I had just come down to see my Grandmother. Then I looked at him sideways. He instantly cut me a look and said,

"We got problems young one?"

I looked back at him and asked him with sincerity,

"Did you get my mom locked up?" He looked surprised.

"Why would you ask me something like that?" Whether you know it or not, I loved your mom. Don't listen to these fools out here Bake."

He told me that a lot of people were jealous because they were trying to figure out how his country a&& got with a true beauty like my mother.

"Believe half of what you see and none of what you hear," he said.

He then shook my hand, hood style and walked back to his car. As he was pulling off he shot me this look. It was different from the normal smirk. This one was more serious. He looked like he was hurt. SHT! I think the NGHA was telling the truth!

The first day of school was coming in a couple of days. That's all we talked about. Aunt Marisa and Mr. Maurice threw the dope cookouts every year in Grandma Rosa's back yard on Labor Day. This year was special for the crew because Aunt Marisa let Sammy and I invite who ever we wanted. Being at our cookouts was like being VIP. We flossed by inviting some of the other kids we use to hustle video games to. It was our way of looking out, and being the hustlers we were, we even sold invites to people because to be at the party meant you had bragging rights. Sammy, Clarkboy, and Hawk invited some of the neighborhood girls. They were even fixing plates for them. I have to admit it; their game was real gangster.

After the girls indulged in a belly full of fried shrimp, lobster, the biggest burgers ever seen, they cuddled by the back fence with the crew. Labor Day weekend gave me another gift and wrapped it in a fly package. Park Place/Colonial Place was known for its fly females. We had had the dopiest girls in our hood and no other matched their swagger, but this one was top of her class. She was banging! Her body was all that, 5'2 about 115 pounds, black silky hair, perky breast, and a backside that was adult like. She had eyes like a cat, and most thought she was mixed with Korean or something. She was beautiful.

Her name was Daja. They called her Day-Day for short. We both were 12 years old; she went to Blair also and was the talk of school from 6th to 8th Grade. Sam walked up to me and told me to take a picture or go and to talk to her. I guess I was staring at her that long and didn't realize it. She was mesmerizing. All of the girls in the pack with Daja heard Sammy and started laughing. I was embarrassed. Sammy got me on that day because I didn't know how to spit game to girls. He called me out!

I was use to girls' salivating over my Dominican features and coming to me. Light skinned curly hair dudes were in back then. My aunt said I had the Al B. Sure look pumping and that drove the chicas wild.

I started walking away because he wasn't about to play me out like that. I then heard,
"I guess I wasn't worth the picture frame?"
I turned around and Daja was right in my face.
"What you mean by that?" I asked.
"You were taking pictures of me with your eyes and you left without framing me."
I had no clue to what the hell she was taking about. I was real green when it came to the talk game with girls but I played like I had swag.
"I can frame you now?"

She smiled and walked towards the front of the house. We sat on the porch and talked while drinking red kool-aid like it was wine. I loved our conversation. I was very comfortable around Daja. She told me about her life. Ours were similar. She lived with her Grandfather because her mom was murdered when she was six years old and her Dad was strung out on heroin. Park Place/Colonial Place was known for Grandparents raising their grandchildren because the influence of the streets. It was a black hole and anything that came near was sucked in. Being children in a hood like that, all you could do is just live and ride the torrent winds the best you could.

As we left we were ushered off with giggles from the adults that over heard the conversation. On the front porch, we talked until the sun became tired and was ready to lay it down. Daja's voice was angelic. I didn't want it to end, but her sister Tasha had to go, so I made sure I got her number so I could call her later.

We all walked the girls' home. As we were leaving, Daja looked at me and said,

"You know if you place me in a gold frame it will last forever."

With that one line she had me! The crew joke me the whole way home. When we got back Mr. Maurice gave us all twenty dollars apiece to clean up the back yard. We took the money and all started laughing. The money he gave us was nothing compared to what we made with Big Sippi.

All of the grownups said their good-byes to grand and headed back to Aunt Marisa's apartment for the adult part of the cookout. Sammy stayed at the house with me because the next day was the first day of school. The rest of the crew went to their cribs, but not before chanting our crew call, a long, delayed, and loud...NOIZEEEE! That was our greeting and farewell.

Sammy and I prepared for the next day.

"Bake you ready," he said with the biggest smile on his face.

"Hells yeah," I replied, and then I followed it with I trade mark greeting...NOIZE! We then walked in grand's room and ask was there anything she wanted us to do before bed.

"Yes, say your prayers before you lay down," she said ever so gently, and then gave us five dollars each for lunch. We once again smiled because of the money, and then went to my room.

Actually the twenty-five dollars, plus the dough we made from selling invites was cool. I just added it to the rest of the money I made from the block.

Early that morning we were awaken by the sound of Tito Puente, the smell of fresh fruit, eggs, and pancakes. Grandmother Rosa was always an early morning person. I loved my grandmother's cooking. When we got to the table, we were greeted by a super breakfast fit for a king. After breakfast, Sammy and I gathered our books and proceeded out the door to walk to school. Before we left, grand gave us both a kiss, and said,

"Trouble is easy to walk into, so move cautiously." She then smiled and walked back towards the sink to wash the dishes. In a way we were shook, because grand had a lot of wisdom and saw a lot of the future.

On our way to school, Sammy and I met up with the crew. We were all fly. Everyone was rocking a fresh pair of blue and white suede Adidas, blue jeans and a blue Adidas tee shirt. Big Sippi had brought all of us gear a week before school. You couldn't say anything to us. We were the center of attention. All day long, all you heard over the whole school was, NOIZE! We influenced almost an entire school in one day. Everyone wanted to be us, and every chic wanted to be with us.

My first class was Social Studies. I waited to the warning bell before I proceeded in because I wanted to make an entrance. Once I reach the classroom door, I heard our call. It was Swampman and Tony. I knew it was going to be all that. As I was sitting down I heard a beautiful voice say,

"You have that gold frame yet?"

I smiled because I knew that heavenly voice. I turned around and sitting right behind me was Daja. She was dressed to kill! She was rocking a jean Jordache skirt with the ruffles socks and pumps.

"I'll have it by the end of this semester." I said in a supposedly sexy tone.

"You think." She said sarcastically.

"Without a doubt ma!" I said with more confidence.

Forty-five minutes later the bell rung and we left our first class. I walked out with Swampman and Tony.

"I guess your boys get framed first."

She walked passed me with her girls and rolled her eyes as she left. She looked mad but I couldn't tell if she was or just being funny. I knew it was time to jump on my chance before I lost it!

A couple of hours later the lunch bell rung. This was the moment I was waiting for. The lunchroom was the showroom and I was ready to walk in with Swampman and Tony, so we could floss. Sammy, Clarkboy, and Hawk were on the third lunch shift with the 8th graders, but it was okay. Half of the "Noize Makers" was together, and that's all that mattered. Once in the lunchroom, we were marveled at like new cars on a showroom floor. Our table was the spot, and they all wanted to eat with us. Tony purchased ice cream for the whole table. It was like fifteen people at our table. That took our status to a higher level.

"Ease up a Tone, remember what Big Sippi told us," Swampman said within a serious manner.

Big Sippi had a conversation with us one day. He told us to watch how we spend money or the goons will. Tony said out loud,

"My mom is going to kill me if I spend all my money for the week."

We both looked at each other and smiled because we knew that through a monkey wrench in everything they were thinking. He said to me in private,

"One day they gone know and we ain't going to be able to hide it."

Tony walked back to the table after that. I thought about what he said. He was right because sooner or later the world was going to know if things kept flowing like they were.

I didn't see Daja until after lunch. She was walking out of the backdoor, and I quickly approached her before she left. "Daja, why didn't you come to the table?"

"That circus, I didn't want to look like a groupie."

"Never that, I don't see you that way."

She smiled and I then walked her to class. After school, the whole crew was on our way home.

Sammy told everyone to come over his house first so he could put his books up. We were going to go to Stuart Elementary and play basketball but when we got to the house, the cops were everywhere. They had the entire apartment building surrounded. One of the cops yelled

"Get those kids the hell back."

Sam replied, "I live here!"

One of the cops immediately came to Sam and said, "What's your mother's name?" "Is her name Marisa Grimes?"

"Yeah, that's my mom, what's going on."

The cop then pulled Sammy to the side away from the crew and start talking to him alone. We were in suspense. None of us knew what was going on, and then Sammy's whole facial expression was blank. The blank facial expression made it hard for us to read the situation. Clarkboy thought we had got popped. None of us ever seen anything, or even held any money so it couldn't be us.

"Maybe it got something to do with my Aunt Marisa or Mr. Maurice?"

We all came up with our theories about what was going on, but we were clueless. About twenty minutes went by, and the cops were still interrogating Sammy. Five more minutes passed and Sammy finally walked back over to us.

"Man this is crazy, some goons got my mom and Mr. Maurice hemmed up inside!"

"They got Aunt Marisa, what you mean primo?"

He told us the cops got a call of a loud disturbance coming from the crib when they got there, they found out some goons had Aunt Marisa and Mr. Maurice hostage in the house. Aunt Marisa's neighbor, Ms Peaches walked over to us.

"I heard 'em when they came in, they were all laughing and joking at first, I don't understand baby."

We all looked at her, because we still were lost about what was happening also. She walked away without filling us in with more details.

About two hours went passed, and the cops were still at a stalemate with those punks who had my aunt. Out of frustration, I started walking down 35th street, towards Granby Street. When I got to 35th and Llewellyn, I saw Big Sippi driving toward the stoplight at the corner.

"Bake get in the car, where is your cousin, and the rest of the Noize Makers?"

"They down by the crib."

"Get in Bake; let's go get 'em and talk."

I got in the car, and he drove back down Llewellyn Avenue and took a left on 37th street. He then stopped at the corner of 37th and Debree. He told me to go get the crew and meet him back at the corner. I got out, ran up Debree like Flash Gordon, and told the crew. We all raced down the block were Big Sippi was parked. He told us to walk to City Park, and meet him in the back by the picnic area. We all streaked away like lighting to City Park, ducking cars, and screaming drivers. Once there, Big Sippi was sitting on one of the tables and told us to gather around. He proceeded to tell us what was going on.

"They work for Maurice, and they weren't happy because they felt like Maurice was the only one eating."
"What does that got to do with my mom?"
Big Sippi answered, "Wrong place, wrong time!"
"This is the issue; the other cats from the same crew are on to us so we got problems."
We all were shook.
"Are they coming for us next?" Tony asked? Big Sippi nodded his head slowly up and down.
"What we 'gone do?" Hawk asked.
Big Sippi then said,
"Ya'll gone to have to grow up real fast!"
"What the hell you mean?" Sammy said with rage in his voice.
"Time to strapped up and get tough my NGHA!" Big Sippi replied.
"I know where they beat. We got to get them before they get us." Big Sippi told us we had to do the unthinkable; murder! We all weren't with it.
"It's got to be another way," I said.
All of a sudden the sporadic sound of gunfire filled the Park Place air. Sammy jumped and screamed "MAMA!" We all then dashed from the park. We ran non-stop back to Aunt Marisa's. All I was thinking was auntie and Mr. Maurice was dead. We got in front of the apartment building, and cops were at an all out war with two the goons the Huntersville boys sent after Mr. Maurice. They screamed for us to get back. When the fight was over, two cops and the boys from Huntersville were dead. I couldn't do anything else, but think the worst about auntie and

Mr. Maurice. The swat team came out of the building and shook his head at the paramedics, and then he belted, "CLEAR THE WAY!" By this time the cops had the yellow tape around the building. We all waited frantically to see if auntie and Maurice would come down walking or on a gurney bed. We then heard the paramedics scream, "She's alive!" They rushed aunt into the ambulance and let Sammy go with 'em.

"Tell Grand what's up Bake."

I couldn't stop crying. I was scared. As the rest of the crew and as I were leaving, we heard another cop say Mr. Maurice was dead!

Baker Grimes
Hamza Atoi
CHAPTER TWO

We continued walking towards Colonial Place. Once at my house, grand was sitting on the porch reading. She saw the look on our face.

"Is that fiasco down there involving you all?"

"Grand!" I said crying franticly, "Auntie Marisa and Mr. Maurice were ambushed. Mr. Maurice is dead and she's on the way to the hospital."

"You boys come in." We walked in slowly, hunched over with our heads hanging low. She then asked me where was Sammy

"He's at the hospital with auntie." She was shot in the chest."

She didn't drop a tear. She told the crew to call their parents so they would know they're ok. Grandma Rosa then got on the phone with the hospital to find out the status of auntie's gunshot wound. She came back to the kitchen with good news.

"Your aunt is just fine."

We all smiled and start wiping our tears. Later, Tony's father came and picked everyone up and we went to Norfolk General Hospital to see Aunt Marisa. We arrived at the hospital quickly. We saw Sammy and Big Sippi sitting quietly with their heads hanging low. Big Sippi stood up and gave Grand his seat next to Sammy.

"Hello Ms. Rosa, longtime no see."

Grand spoke back and hugged him like one of her own.

"Dear boy, where have you been?"

"I've been around Ms. Rosa. It just hurts to see you because... you...you know."

"Don't let that stop you. Pain heals after time."

She sat down and ended the conversation by telling Big Sippi he was always welcome.

"Thank you Ms. Rosa," he replied, got up and walked to the phone. I could read the look on his face. He was ready to handle business. Aunt Marisa was his road dog. He looked out for her like she was his sister. I think he wanted payback just as bad as we did.

Hours had passed before we were able to see auntie. Big Sippi stayed the whole entire time with us. The doctor came down and told us Aunt Marisa was fine, but she needed her rest. He said it would be better if we came back tomorrow, so Big Sippi took us home. Grand thanked him and asked if he wanted something to eat.

"No thank you Ms. Rosa. I need to be getting home. I have a long day ahead of me tomorrow." You could see the fire building in his eyes. It was revenge time!

Once in the house, Sammy and I immediately walked upstairs to my room. For about an hour we didn't talk. The silence was as cold as a Boston winter. The room was filled with thoughts and I could smell the sulfur of satan's breath on the side of my ear. Driving my thoughts into an area I had never dealt in. I got on my bed, rolled on my back and stared at the ceiling like it had the answer I was looking for. I was going over the thought of murder over and over in my head, and then Sammy spoke.

"I miss Mr. Maurice already! You knew what we have to do Bake?" Sammy asked already answering his own question with his look.

"What?" I said with naivety

"We have to get them Huntersville chumps!"

Sammy said he talked to Big Sippi about it before Grand and I got to the Hospital.

"We are going to set them up."

The ones who setup the entire sting lived on C Ave. They thought they were going to make a pick up for one of the big wheels out the Ville named "Do-Wop." Do-Wop ran all of the work in and out of "The Parks" (Virginia term for projects) in Norfolk and all of Huntersville. Do-Wop took over the empire from his cousin who was serving Fed time for his involvement in the drug trade in Norfolk. They had their part of the city on lock! They were part of the main players in the Norfolk drug trade and one of the deadliest also! Do-Wop was down because his cousin younger cousin "Fame was robbed by the same stick up crew that murdered Mr. Maurice and wounded Aunt Marisa. Fame was his little prodigy and even deeper; it was his Fam!

"Big Sippi got with Do-Wop to make it all happen." Sammy said.

Sammy then rolled over and told me to get some rest because after school tomorrow they were going to be dead! I tried but I couldn't sleep. I didn't want to murder anyone. My mom was a stone cold killer, but that didn't mean I could do it. To be a murderer you had to be cold blooded and I didn't have that kind of heart.

After about an hour of contemplation, I was finally able to go to sleep. That morning Sammy woke me up before the sea started to give birth to the sun. He had pure electricity in his eyes. He was definitely ready. We went to school that day, and met up with the Noize makers. Everyone was looking like scared rabbits besides Sammy. By those facial expressions they must have known what was going to happen after school. The tension in the air was thick.

"This is going to be for my Mom and Maurice, Noize!" Sammy belted from his gut with pure anger. The day went by fast. I guess it was the anticipation. The final bell rang, and we all met up, and walked to Park Place to meet Big Sippi. When we arrived at our destination we saw Big Sippi sitting in his car. On the outside of his driver side door was this big, black gorilla looking. Big Sippi spoke and introduced his henchman named, "Schizoid." This NGHA was huge. He didn't smile once nor did he speak when we spoke to him. He had the demeanor of a true killer.

Big Sippi told us he was going to drop us off at this spot on Reservoir Ave. When we got there we enter this old broken down home that looked like it was abandoned. I was really losing my composure on the inside but I held it very well. When we got inside it smiled like someone had already died. It was spooky looking like the contents of a Stephen King novel. We all didn't say a word. We consumed by the thought of what was about to happen. They left and about an hour later we heard a rumbling sound at the back door. We kept quiet because we didn't know whom it was. Then we heard,

"Aye Yo Noize! Let's handle this SHT!"

It was now, Big Sippi, Schizoid, and two other diesel looking characters. They had the dudes from Huntersville tied up. They were placed in two steel folding chairs. The fear seeped from the backside of their jeans proving they knew they were in deep SHT! They were shaking worse than a "Tailgaters" stripper whose body was riddled with stretch marks and bullet wounds on their thick, cellulite filled a&&.

"Y'all ready, you ready Sammy, we gone work these NGHA's!"

Before whatever brutal plan Big Sippi had was about to be fulfilled, there was a knock at the door. It was Do-Wop and Fame. Big Sippi let 'em in, and Do-Wop immediately asked if we had started yet.

"Hell no Do-Wop, Y'all right on time."

Fame was about our age, but that dude was standing like he was trained to go. He had two 38 revolvers in his hand that he pulled from his waist. Big Sippi then went into a brown bag and pulled out some box cutters. He then told us all to grab one. Big Sippi then went over and whispered something to Do-Wop, and then Do-Wop whispered to Fame. Fame then walked over to Sammy, passed him one of the 38's, and then whispered in his ear. Country started screaming,

"This is my family, my sons. You don't FCK with a man's family. Y'all grown men, these are kids, but we gone show ya'll NGHAS today"

Schizoid and Big Sippi's other two henchman began beating the crap out of one of them. They beat him so bad his teeth were laying on the plastic that Big Sippi had under each chair. After they gave the most vicious beat down I had ever seen in my life, Schizoid immediately started working on the other guy. He was throwing punches so hard you could hear the wind follow each swing. The landing punches sounded like thunder. Each blow roared as they approached. We all stood there with our eyes locked on the malicious assault being inflicted. It ended after a brutal and savage beating was imposed. The two stick up boys responsible for what happen to Aunt Marisa and Mr. Maurice slumped over in their chairs. Their bodies were as close to death as one could come while still breathing. Big Sippi then told each one of us to give them both two slashes apiece. One slash was for Maurice and one for Aunt Marisa. No one hesitated. Hawk went first hitting both in the face twice, followed by Swampman, Clarkboy, and then Tony. It was my turn. I paused for a brief second then something in me snapped. I hit the first one behind the ear and struck a second blow beneath his bottom lip, and then I put in an all out assault on the second dude. I was slashing him so much I had blood all over my body. Big Sippi had to grab me to stop me. I looked at the near death bodies with a demonic stare. It even made Schizoid grimaced. Big Sippi then looked at Fame and Sammy. They raised their guns. Sammy was in front of one, and Fame was in front of the other one. They took aim and one behind the other, fired the fatal blow that ended the lives. Schizoid grabbed the guns and box cutters, placed them in a plastic wrap, put them in a book bag and walked out. Big Sippi gave a handshake to Do-Wop and Fame as they left.

The room was silent. Big Sippi took me in the bathroom to wash the blood from my face. He never said a word and neither did I. We just stared at each other. After all of us cleaned ourselves up and changed our clothes, Big Sippi got one of his boys to take us home. The ride home was also silent. Everyone was spaced out. Sammy and I were dropped off first. We said peace to the crew, and went inside the house. The time was about six o' clock pm. Grandma Rosa was in the kitchen sitting at the table reading her bible. She then spoke and asked where had we been? Sammy said immediately and without a second thought,

"We stayed after school to try out for the basketball team."

"I hope you both make it, but next time call me and let me know where you are if you are going to be late. I left food on the stove. I'm going to the hospital to see Marisa."

She told us to clean the dishes after we ate and finish our homework. Sammy asked if he could go with her.

"Sure Poppy, you can come if you like. Baker, you might as well come along also, there is no sense to leave you here alone."

Grand called a cab and within 15 minutes, the cab arrived, and we proceeded to Norfolk General Hospital. When we approached the front desk, Grand asked the secretary for Aunt Marisa's room number. As we approached her door, we heard laughing. It was Big Sippi and Aunt Marisa. They were having a ball it seemed. He stood up and hugged Grand then gave Sammy and I a pound. It felt awkward. Grandmother sat down beside Aunt Marisa and asked how she was doing.

"Just fine Mama. Are those boys giving you a hard time?"

"Not my babies, I never have problems with my little boys."

We both looked at Aunt Marisa and smiled. Sammy walked towards his mother and gave her a big hug. I then began to start laying jokes

"In a few minutes, she's going to put us out and make us go play in the parking lot until she falls asleep." Everyone laughed hard.

"Yeah, I should make you clean this floor, you're lucky I'm in here." The laughs continued, and during the time of our visit with Aunt Marisa, I forgot about what happen earlier that day. Visiting hours was coming to an end. We all said our goodbyes to Auntie and left. Big Sippi took us home again. Once we got home, he kissed Grand on the cheek, and then he said peace to Sammy and I. As he was driving off we heard... Noize! We smiled and walked in the house. Our chest was full of pride. We did the unthinkable. We took the lives of two human beings. No matter what they did they were still someone's son and grandchild. My heart was torn for the moment.

It had been a long day so we went in Grand's room and her. In my room it looked darker than usual. We were sleepy, but neither Sam nor I was asleep.

"Yo Sammy, Are you awake?"

"Yeah I'm up. What's wrong Bake?"

I asked him did he think that we would go to hell for what happened today. He said he didn't think so because we had no choice.

"It was either them or us Bake."

I laid there thinking about what he said.

"What if you don't feel bad about it? Do you think God will forgive us?"

"Of course he will Bake, he knew the situation, and we didn't have a choice. Those guys were going to kill us because we were getting money."

"You think that is a sign we should get out. We not hustlers Sammy! We just kids who want to have fun! This is getting out of control."

I don't think Sammy was trying to hear it because he didn't answer. In my eyes we weren't built for the life we were growing into. The day of the murders showed me how serious it was and I really wanted out. The room was silent for bout ten minutes. He then told me to get up so we could pray and ask God for forgiveness for it. We got off our beds and kneeled down, and Sammy led our plea for repentance. The whole time was strange. I wasn't remorseful about what happened. I felt cold hearted, and because of it I felt hypocritical about praying for forgiveness, so I just went through the motions. After we prayed, we climbed back in our beds and went to sleep.

Just like every morning when we awoke, we were greeted with beautiful orchestrated drums of Tito Puente and the fresh smell of breakfast. We washed our bodies, put on our clothes, and went downstairs to partake in the glory that was spread magnificently across the table. Beside both our plates was a ten-dollar bill. I asked Grand the dumbest and uncalculated question. It led to her to start investigating.

"Grand, what's the money for?"

"Since you and Sammy hadn't been asking for it, I thought you two needed it. Am I wrong?"

"No Grandma Rosa, we had...um...we were just so wrapped up in school we didn't ask for it."

"School must be interesting for the both of you this year," she replied.

"You two aren't doing anything that you are not suppose to, are you?" We both answered simultaneously, "No!" She smiled, sat down, and then said, "I don't worry about you two boys." She then called us her lil Santos.

"Just listen to your Abuela, I won't steer you wrong, si?"

"Si, Abuela Rosa.

We kissed Grand, and went off to school. The weekend was approaching. After school we all got together at my house and plotted our next moves. Swampman led off the conversation.

"Man, we smashed the hell out them cats!" Clarkboy then replied, "I know but it ain't nothing to brag over."

"Yo, we're murderers!"

I was silent the whole conversation.

"Bake, why you not talking?"

"I'm good." I just didn't want to talk about what happened. It wasn't cool to take a life Tone!

Sammy then said to Hawk,

"You hit that dude so deep; I thought you were trying to do surgery."

"I just thought about your moms, and it just pissed me off." Hawk replied.

He then began to brag about me.

"Y'all see my primo? He thought he was an in Jason movie or something!"

All of us started laughing because of the way Sammy imitated me and how I hit them dudes up. Sammy then stuck his hand out and said, "I love y'all!" "Y'all held me and Bake down, I appreciate that."

Clarkboy replied, "It ain't nothing, we crew right?" He was right. We were official. The ordinary little kids who hustled video games were now beginning the most notorious crew Park Place would ever see.

Baker Grimes
Hamza Atoi
CHAPTER THREE

From the time we murdered those two stick-up boys from *the village* up until the summer was boring so let me fast forward for you.

The summer had once again arrived, and Aunt Marisa had recovered well from her gunshot wounds, but things began to move in a different motion on the block. With disregard to all the things that happen, we still went back full- time in front of Red ball, but a lot of changes were made because of this new drug that hit Park Place.

Crack cocaine hit the streets like a pit-bull hitting the neck of a poodle. Now there were two major drugs in our hood, and that put out extra heat. Big Sippi had to set things up a lot different because "crack heads" as we called them walked the streets every fifteen minutes. "Dope heads," were starting to use crack too. We knew eventually that we were going to have to move from Red ball, and switch to one of the apartments. I thought that was better anyway because we were getting too old to continue playing in front of the corner store.

Before crack hit the block, the traffic was controlled because the high of diesel lasted longer. Heroin addicts would cop and go, but it was something about the high of crack that had them coming back like every 15 to 20 minutes. They would sell their kids for a hit. I knew it wouldn't take long before Big

Sippi ceased the chance to put his hand in the crackpot. Our customers were starting to speedball instead of just of just banging their bodies up with tracks. They were sniffing and smoking stems, and got a better high.

For a while we continued to move product in front of Red ball. We pushed both heroin and crack cocaine. Big Sippi even boosted our pay because we went from runners and watchers to dealing with the product ourselves, but most of the money was put in a safe for us. We had trust in him, so it was cool. He didn't want us to hold on to too much money because we were still kids, and you know how kids are with money. It would've burned our pockets. Big Sippi kept records along with us about the amount of money we had in the safe. He also put 10% of it to the side in case of an emergency like one of us getting locked. He had it all taking care of. We didn't have to want for anything.

Big Sippi purchased a duplex apartment for Aunt Marisa. No one lived in it but us. He wasn't slick. He had it all set up for a sole purpose.

The Crew moved product on the block like an assembly line. It got to a point where we had to have an open and close time. Big Sippi taught us how not to be greedy. He said the money that we lost when shop was closed was nothing and to let the crumb eaters have it. This was also done so that greed and envy wouldn't take place because everyone was able to eat well. We were still kids anyway so we couldn't hang out but so late. We had to keep our identities concealed from the passing police. Aunt Marisa knew what was going on by this time, but she was about that money, and Mr. Maurice wasn't there to give it to her, so we had free reign to do as we pleased.

During all this wheeling and dealing, I was wondering what my mom would say if she knew. I thought about her a lot. I rarely was able to see her because they had moved her to an upstate prison. She had been there since I was seven years old. Her and Grand didn't really see eye-to-eye then because Mama Maria wanted to see me every weekend, but grand said it wasn't logical since we didn't have a car. Mama Maria resented Grandma Rosa for it. I never saw my mom after she left the Goose land women facility. She had fed and state time to fulfill so she was moved to several different facilities before her last stop. It was somewhere in Connecticut.

I sent pictures, but I never received mail of any sort from her. It had been about five years since I heard anything from my mother. She didn't call or write any one. It made me a little bitter and resentful, but I had to put myself in her shoes. One thing I did know; I missed her a lot. I often wondered what she was thinking. I wondered if she had any thoughts about anything outside of prison and did it really even matter. I immediately put it out of my head because thoughts of my mom always put me in a deep depression. I put my thoughts back on the block, and that money that we were getting.

I rarely stayed at home with Grandma Rosa. Most of my time was spent at Aunt Marisa's because there I had no curfew, but Sammy and I made sure that we made visits to Grand every day. All of our time was

Baker Grimes/Hamza Atoi

spent in Park Place. That's all we knew. I remember when Big Sippi planned a trip with the Colonial boys & club to go to Bush Gardens in Williamsburg, VA. We were hyped because none of us had ever been to a real theme park before. The only one was at Military Circle Mall, and that was an amusement park that came every other summer.

All you needed was a signed permission slip from your parents. Big Sippi had already paid for the whole trip; food included. I saw this as an opportunity to spend some quality time with Daja. We were able to see each other sometimes, but her grandfather wasn't seeing any guys sitting over his house, on his porch, gaming to his granddaughters. It was not happening, so most of the time the only way we were able to send time was if she went to the recreation center or the boys club.

On the block we all worked in four-hour shifts, two at a time so I spent all the time I could with her since our time was limited. This trip would give me a whole day with her, and I was looking ill as hell. The day before, Big Sippi took us shopping. We went to Military Circle Mall, and picked up the new Tretons, some Duck head Pants and a couple Ralph Lauren Polo's. While we were there, I purchased Daja this gold 14kt gold ¾ inch Herringbone. I wanted to hit her off with a ring too, but I didn't want to take it too far. Sammy and I went pass McCory's and took some pictures to give to Grand and I took some solo joints to give to Daja. I was fly and shinning like new money.

The morning had finally arrived, and we were ready to have a ball. We all met up at Aunt Marisa's. Everyone except Swampman was there. Hawk said he called Swampman before he left to meet us but no one answered. Swampman's family was on some next SHT every now and then. He was always in the middle of his stepfather and mother's domestic disputes. We all went over to Swamp man's house before we left to walk to the boy's club, but no one answered. He must have gone over to his grandmother's. We all went over to the Boys club so that we could prepare for the trip to Bush Gardens. It was five minutes before leaving time, and still no Swampman. Big Sippi came on the bus and asked where he was. We had no answers for him, so he said,

"Well, we have to ride, we'll see him when we get back" I was ready for the trip, but I wished that Swampman was there with us because Noize did everything together.

Bush Gardens was the bomb like always. We ate everything from funnel cake, lemon pie, cotton candy, and huge German hot sausages. We rode rides, screamed, and won all of the prizes that the park had to offer. Daja and I laughed, cuddled, and kissed after every ride and game. We had so many stuffed animals we had to take them back to the bus.

The day of super fun quickly came to an end. It was time to leave the land of excitement and travel back to the streets of Park Place. The trip home was over too quick also. I wanted to sit and hold Daja a little longer. The next thing I know, we were stopping in front of the Boys Club. Once there her Grandfather was waiting so I said my good-byes from a distance, and told her to call me later. It was kind of late. It was about 10 PM when we got home. The shop was closed for the day, so we had time just to chill. Big Sippi took the rest of the crew to their separate homes. Hawk lived the closet to Swampman so he said he would check on him to make sure everything was o.k.

Sammy and I stayed at Aunt Marisa's. It was late, so I decided to go to bed. I was tired from that day's activity, but before I could lie down and rest, I got a phone call from Daja. I was excited to hear her voice, but her voice wasn't normal, she sound disturbed. "What's wrong Day-Day?"

She was quiet for a minute then she asked me if I heard. I replied, "heard what?" "Swamp man was on the news." They said he murdered his stepfather, and they got him at Norfolk Detention home". My mouth dropped, and then the phone beeped. "Day hold on, I got somebody on the other end." I answered the phone, and it was Hawk on the other line. "Bake, did you hear about what happened?" "Yeah, I'm talking to Daja about it now. I'll hit you right back." I clicked the phone back over to Day, and told her, I would call her back. Sammy was outside, so I ran downstairs from the apartment, and dashed out the door to tell Sammy what happened. "Sammy!" I screamed,   "Come in, I have to tell you something important". He had this long look on his face. I knew then that he knew.

He was outside talking to this old head that we knew named Kimbo. Kimbo lived next door to Swampman and said that he heard the whole thing. We asked him when it happened, and he said last night, but that wasn't all. Swampman's mother was also dead. His father apparently stabbed his mom up, and then Swampman walked in and lit his step pops up. I knew one day it would happen because Swampman hated his stepfather. He would always say when we were younger that he was going to kill him one day. His step pops was off the hook. He would beat Swampman when he was a little kid for spilling milk on the table, and then beat Swampman's mom if she had anything to say about.

By now, everyone in Park Place knew so half of the cats we knew were in front of Sammy's apartment. It was the news of the day, but we shut things down real fast and just left them outside by themselves. None of them were crew so we weren't going to sit there and listen to the gossip. Sammy and I went to in the crib. We were hurting because Swampman's mom was like a second mom to all of us. We weren't worrying about Swampman handling lock up because we knew he was built tough like a Tonka truck. We were worrying about his emotional state. Seeing your mother stabbed up is a hard thing to deal with.

Before we went to bed, Sammy and I said a prayer for Swampman and his mom. As far as we were concerned his dad could rot in hell. The next morning, we all got together for work, but the tension was high. We had work to do regardless of it all.

There was nothing we could do for him anyway because he was being held without bond. All we could do was make sure that he had a good lawyer.

The whole day was moving slow. There wasn't a lot of conversation. Kimbo walked pass again to talk to us. Kimbo was a dope addict we served, but he was always cool. He taught us a lot about the streets on our way up.

"Y'all kids ok?"

Everyone gave a low and depressed yes.

"He's gone be alright young ones, so don't you all worry; the lord got him in his arms".

Then he walked down the street to wherever he was going. Kimbo was always a good person, even when he was doing dope. He was one of the only addicts we felt bad serving because he always had something good to say to us. When we first started on the block in front of Red ball, Kimbo use to give us encouraging words about school. He was always concerned, and that was unlike the others who just wanted their fix. We all liked him.

The night was finally coming to an end. The whole crew minus Swampman had worked the entire 8 hours together. Tony, Hawk, and Clarkboy spent the night over Aunt Marisa's so that made it easy to do the all day hustle without their parents looking for them. We didn't do much that night, but play the new Nintendo that Grandma Rosa bought for Sammy and I. We were in the middle of a serious Tecmo bowl tournament when the phone rang. Sammy jumped up and answered it on the first ring. "Hello?" His face grew into an ear-to-ear smile. We all knew it was

Swampman. Sammy talked to him for a minute. And then let everyone say what's up to him. He let us now that he was cool, but down in spirits.

Sammy talked to him the majority of the time. He told Sammy most of the story, but he said he would call back and tell us the rest later because he needed to call his grandmother. We all said good-bye, and waited with anticipation for him to call back. Sammy began to tell us what Swampman told him.

He went on to say Swampman said he was in his room, and his step pop barged in and asked if he could hold something. Swampman replied "hold what?" He then said that his step pops start wilding and begin to tear up his room, rambled through his things while saying "I know you holding let me hold something. All of the commotion woke his mom and she walked in to see what was going on.

"You know this lil punk selling drugs, you know your sweet lil son hustling with his pissy lil friends." Swampman's mother then asked,

"Why are you tearing up his room?

"I don't want it in my house!"

He told his mom that his pops was lying and he came in asking me out the blue could he hold something. He said that's when it took off, but that's all he was able to tell me because his counselor said he had only five minutes left and he wanted to use the rest of the time to talk to his grandmother. We had to wait until for him to call back to hear the rest.

Clarkboy jumped up and said, "Now that I remember, I use to see Swampman's pops with Kimbo. He was always with him when Kimbo use to

cop." I then told the crew that I had an idea that something was up because would always call all of us the little peewee runners. He would then say the exact thing that Swampman said he said to him, "Let me hold something fresh money."
Everything was making sense now, but I wondered why Swampman never said anything. He probably didn't know. We talked all night while waiting for Swampman to call back, but we never received the call. After a long conversation, and even longer games of Tecmo bowl, we all finally went to sleep. The next day, the rest of the crew went home, and Sammy and I worked the shift alone. We sat outside talking about Swampman the entire time. There was kid from the hood we didn't care for too much because he always hated on us. He was a punk we called, "Snitch" because in school he was always telling on people. He would snitch on you about anything.
"Aye Yo let me get a cap?" Snitch said arrogantly.
"NGHA what?" Sammy replied.
"Let me get one of them red tops from you?" I then told him to get gone because there wasn't anything popping off. He left saying something under his breath. I smelled setup. I jumped off the fence and start looking around because I remember when Big Sippi told us that when he first started, the older heads would use him to set people up. I told Sammy to keep his eyes open. Before shift change Hawk and Tony came through. I told them about our encounter with Snitch and Hawk immediately said,
"Naw yo, he ain't trying to set up a NGHA, he on that Diesel for real."

We all asked almost at the same time, how he knew. He replied, he been coping from me for the past month. Everyone looked at Hawk in shock, and then Sammy said,

"You know you don't suppose to be pushing on the side, you know the rules."

"I wasn't hurting Noize money, we gone get what we get regardless of that lil money."

That wasn't the point. Big Sippi told us from jump to stay getting money as a family, no outside hustling. He did this for a reason. He did it to monitor us because we were still kids, and there was a lot of the game that we didn't know. That's how we all could get set up because Snitch could be setting Hawk up, and then his heat could become ours. As a crew we were safe because we weren't in the dark about anything.

Hawk apologized and promised that he wouldn't hustle outside the crew anymore. See the way Big Sippi had it setup, we were protected because all we touched was money. Immediately after we got the money it went into a drop box on the side of the spot. The old heads on the inside were never seen, so cops were not able to pin point anyone by constantly seeing their face. The house was only a money house. They had to walk to the end of the block, to another spot to get the product. Big Sippi's set up was sweet, and both spots had straight killers inside, so we weren't worrying about the spot being kicked in by stickup boys. We never kept money on us while we were working so it was pointless. It carried a death sentence to try and stick us.

Baker Grimes
Hamza Atoi
CHAPTER FOUR

A couple of weeks went by and we hadn't heard anything from Swampman. His grandmother told us he was in a fight, so they took away all his privileges. I knew that was going to happen because Swampman was always the type to fire off on you if you disrespected him. All we could do was wait to hear from him, but as we waited, the dominos begin to fall.

In every hood you always have the young addict, who wanted to be down with everything and would try anything. Snitch was our resident adolescent dope head. We heard he got on heroin from an old head that told him he would be able to go all night in the bedroom. He took one hit and was done. It was a rumor the cops had turned him also so we never dealt him anything. We had the best product on the block and everyone knew it. Every time he would come around he would ask where the missiles were. We would all laughed and would tell him they at the Naval Station. He would walk away pissed because those dudes out villa heights had some garbage.

Snitch began to come around every day and every day we sent him packing. We didn't want his money. Big Sippi gave us free reign to turn away anyone we wanted. It was no way we were going to serve him.

Every day he continued to try, and it got to a point where he had to get it. We often wondered where his parents were because this dude was outside morning till night, but where were any of the kids parents in Park Place? That answer was easy; they were coming to see us!

Well to make a long story short about that, we beat the crap out of Snitch, and this is where Karma comes in. Snitch was Fame's little brother. They had the same Father. Yeah, I know you thinking what I think your thinking. You're right! I'm talking about the same Fame that was with us when we put the murder game down on those Huntersville NGHAS. The word on the street him and some "Calvert Park", or as we say "Curry Park" boys was on some hit us up SHT. We didn't take it lightly because we knew Fame was trained to go. We let Big Sippi know what was going because we didn't want any heat to come down on the block. He said he would go talk to Do-Wop, and let him know it was a misunderstanding. Big Sippi got on his cell, and told Do-Wop what happen. His facial expression looked frustrated. He said aggressively

"Do-Wop, this thing gone cost both us money." We looked with anticipation and didn't know what his reply was. After about five minutes of debating Big Sippi said,

"Aight, I can do that to squash it, but keep that lil NGHA away from here or next time we just gone go to war."

He hung up the phone, and told us what was up. He said,

"Since Swampman is gone, I'm gone to let Fame take his spot for a minute." We all had the same feeling. He wasn't Noize we said!

"I didn't say he was Noize, he just going to take Swampman shift for a minute until this tension settles down. Me and Do-Wop got business together."

"I am going to let him" . . . he paused. "This is my shit! Fame is working Swampman shift and that's that."

He jumped in his car and pulled off. We were pissed! We felt that Big Sippi laid down when we were ready for war.

The next day had come. Sammy and I woke up around 7am. Aunt Marisa was still asleep, so we quietly cut on the TV, Nintendo, and while playing the game conversed about the situation. Sammy said he didn't care because he felt Big Sippi wouldn't steer us wrong. I on the other hand hated it because I felt that Noize was Noize. It wasn't a place to take, but Sammy being the wiser one knew it was a money thing. He knew Big Sippi and Do-Wop had to be in business together. I still didn't like it, but I had to accept it.

Hawk and Clarkboy worked the first shift. Tony and I worked the second. Fame and Sammy worked the third. I can't say much about what happened that day because all was quiet. We all sat outside on the block while Fame and Sammy worked their shift. No one spoke to Fame besides Sammy. You could feel the tension and see it in his eyes because Fame was just as mad as us.

The night had finally come to an end and one of Do-Wop's boys had come to pick up Fame. Fame looked at all of us, and said,

"We peace right?" Everybody nodded their head then shook hands, except me. I turned around and walked into Aunt Marisa's apartment building. After a while Sammy came in. He stared at me and then just walked away. I knew he was mad, but I didn't care because regardless of anything Fame wasn't Noize. Sammy and I didn't speak for half the night. I watched TV and he was playing Tecmo Bowl. I decided to break the ice because maybe I was wrong.

"Yo, Sammy."

"What up Bake?" "What you think about Fame?"

"He a cool dude, he aight Bake."

Sammy then said something that made sense. He told me that if the situation was switched around and I was Snitch he would be ready to knuckle up too. He was right so I let it all go . . . for the time being.

Another day had come and for some reason, the cops were rolling hard. Big Sippi decided to shut down shop, so I decided to just chill out with Daja for the rest of the day. I told her to get her Grandfather to drop her and her sister off at the mall because The Noize Makers and I were going to be there. She told me she was going to wear this fly outfit she got from the mall with the money I gave her the week before. I couldn't wait to see how she was dipped. We met at Flipper McCoy's and she was right. She was mad fly.

We were all having fun; the day was going good until we saw Fame. He walked in with some guys from Curry Park. That immediately put me on the defense. He walked up and shook hands with Sammy. They laughed and joked but I had no smiles for that NGHA, but everything was cool. Daja was looking at me because she knew I had hell in my eyes. She then said,

"Baby let's get some pizza."

Daja, her sister and I went to the other side to get some slices. All of a sudden I heard,

"I thought that NGHA was getting money, look at him, he can't even buy a whole pizza. He ain't getting any money!"

I quickly turned around and saw some of the dudes from Curry Park. I then replied,

"Y'all ain't nothing, but a bunch of broke dick riders."

Then one of them rebutted,

"Just like that BTCH you with who was riding my dick the other night."

By that time the Noize Makers and Fame was there. Fame began to curse them out.

"They family now, and if y'all don't like it then we can handle this SHT?" He then came over to me and ask if he could talk to me alone. I agreed, plus Daja's grandfather was outside anyway. I walked out and said good-bye and then Fame and I began to talk. The first thing I said was,

"I ain't got to like you and you ain't got to like me, but for the sake of the business, we aight."

"Damn Bake, I'm the one that should be mad, y'all banged my lil brother up, and I did nothing to y'all in retaliation."

I stood there for a second and thought about it, and he was right. I then apologized to him and we

squashed the beef. Once we got back in Flippers, we saw the crew and the Curry Park boys laughing and playing games together. The one that disrespected me was Lee-Lee. He came to me and apologized, "My bad Bake, I didn't mean it."
"It's all good Lee."
It wasn't but it was until I could make it good. You feel me?
It was 10 p.m. and all of us had to leave because of our curfews. Big Sippi and Do-Wop came to scoop us all up. They were happy to see us connecting and getting to know each other. We all greeted each other up and went our separate ways. Big Sippi was in a mellow monotone voice while taking a pull of his cigar.
"War is only pushed when all else fails."
He was once again correct. No money can be made that way. All of the beef was squashed. Weeks had passed and we were all getting along perfect. It got to the point where Fame was even spending the night with us at Aunt Marisa's. Fame was a cool dude.
We still hadn't heard anything from Swampman. We spoke with his grandmother, but she said that she rarely talks to him because he stays in trouble. I missed him a lot. He was my boy. The school year was going good. The block was hot but it was moving. Daja and I were still kicking it.
The first day of Swampman's trial we all got a rude awakening. The prosecutor began to paint the picture, making Swampman look like a savage, out of control kid. He said Swampman maliciously murdered his step pops because he wouldn't let him

go outside and hang with his friends, whom where known for causing trouble. Sammy looked at us because the Prosecutor was talking about us. The Commonwealth attorney also said that he had proof that Swampman did it with a premeditated intent. We all looked at each other wondering what the FCK was happening.

Big Sippi hired a good lawyer from Richmond, but even he was stunned. The first day of opening arguments was over, and we all left the courtroom in dismay. They were trying to railroad Swamp man, and didn't know a thing about his life and what he had been through. His father had it coming.

We all conversed with Swampman's attorney, and he said that Commonwealth attorney had a witness that supposedly heard Swampman and his pops arguing that night. I was rocking my brain trying to figure out who it was. Because of school we weren't able to go to the rest of his trial.

We all caught the Granby Street bus #1 back to Park Place. On the way home all I could think about was the Commonwealth's comments. I was mad because that was far from true. We never caused any trouble around the hood because we were about getting money. I tried to put it out my head once we got home. The whole crew was still talking about it, but I didn't want to hear another word. I went upstairs grabbed my bike and rode to Grandma Rosa's house. Once at Grand', I put my bike on the porch and walked in the house. She wasn't in the kitchen like she normally was. I called franticly for her until I heard her scream downstairs for me to stop my loudness. She was in the room trying to rest and I guess I woke her up with all my yelling. I asked her if she was sick, and she told me that she was tired because she was up all night. Her tone was low, and her eyes were connected with mine. When she spoke and looked the way she did I knew it was an open door for a conversation that was birth from her six senses. Sammy and I were often caught in the mystic trap as we called it, and today were no different.

Since I was already sucked in, I asked why she was up all night. She proceeded to tell me about a dream that she had about the crew and I.

"Last night a vision came and took me to your Auntie's house. It then showed me your path, and it was not good Baker."

I stood in front of her with a face like I saw a demon walk through the room. I was afraid because she looked afraid.

"I see what you do Baker."

And then she told me to remember the conversation we had just had.

"Life has two paths for you, so you have to choose correctly."

She then began to walk downstairs, singing as she walked. I could only stand there in silence. She always knew best, but I was too deep in my eyes, and the money had me trapped.

I went into my room and shook it off and then called down to Auntie's house. I was hoping Sammy was there so I could tell him what was going on, but no one answered the phone. More than likely he was on the block. I sat in the room and began to think. What were the two paths?

Dealing with the visions Grand would have was scary because she was rarely wrong. The path wouldn't be as easy as right or left. I was shook because sometimes the wrong path is the right. By the time I had finished pondering, I heard footsteps coming up the stairs. I didn't realize that it was 10 p.m.

"Are you staying home tonight?"

"Si Abuela"

"Don't let me place fear on you Baker, I know you will choose right little Santo."

She then went into her room. I picked up the phone and called Sammy again, and there was still no answer. I began to panic. I ran in Grand's room and made up a quick lie, so that I could go back to Park Place and see what was going on.

"Grand I forgot Sammy was going to help me study for a test."

"It's late my dear."

"I know hawk and Sammy are going to meet me at the circle."

"They don't need to be out either, but go ahead, make sure you lock the door, and be careful."

I ran down stairs, screamed good-bye, and dashed out the door. I jumped on my bike and flew with the wind behind me to Auntie's house. I feared the worst but when I got there, Sammy, Fame and Kimbo was sitting in the front talking. I spoke to everyone and then everyone spoke back like something was wrong. Sammy then told me that Big Sippi got locked.

"When did he get hit up?" I asked surprised by what I just heard.

Big Sippi locked that was impossible. He never touched anything or let alone had anything near him, so how did he get popped? Fame then said Do-Wop and Big Sippi got locked coming through the Jersey Turnpike. I was thinking this is crazy. Why in the hell would he go through the turnpike, let alone, be in a car with work?

"What's going to happen now?" I asked with great concern because with Big Sippi gone who was gone run things? Sammy and Fame just shrugged their shoulders replying with their body language that they didn't know. This was a low time for us because it took us a while to get back.

Big Sippi and Do-Wop ended with no bond in Jersey, and Swampman was looking at 15 years if they tried him as an adult. The shop ended up shutting down because Big Sippi thought they had us all. He told one of his boys if they ever get him then they got us. They had to have been watching him for a while, so nothing was moving for us. It didn't matter at first because we had G-money saved up. Big Sippi showed us how to save, so money really wasn't a factor. We knew where the safe was with the rest of our money and the lawyer was already paid if we needed him. I think it was more of the lifestyle we would miss the most.

Sammy called a meeting at the house, the next day after school. The meeting was basically about the moves that we needed to make, and since Fame was Part of Noize now, he was part of the meeting also.

When the meeting started, Fame jumped right in and started talking crazy.

"Now that Do-Wop and Big Sippi down, the streets belong to us and we need to take it!

"Big Sippi and Do-Wop not down, you jumping the gun," Sammy said. For about an hour the two of them went back and forth about what needed to be done. I couldn't take it anymore, so I jumped in with my two cents. I should've kept my mouth close, but I couldn't help it. I didn't want Fame in the crew anyway.

"You can't say what Noize gone do because you really ain't Noize anyway!"

The room was at dead silence. All of our progress was thrown out of the window. I made a hasty choice and Fame really was cool. Sammy then told me to apologize, and before I could Fame looked at me with malice in his eyes. "No, it's aight, he right, I ain't Noize for real."

The tension in the room was thick. Clarkboy tried to ease the tension in the room by saying that he was Noize, but Fame wasn't trying to hear it.

"Clarkboy it's cool, I'm just an affiliate that's getting money with you all."

You could tell that Fame was upset because he didn't have anything else to say for the rest of the night. At the end of the night we all came to the conclusion to wait until we heard from Big Sippi. After the meeting Fame got up and said peace to everyone besides me. Hawk then looked at me and said that I was wrong for what I did, and he was right. I ran down the stairs to catch Fame, and when I got down, he was standing in front of the building. I tried to break the ice.

"What up Noize?"

He didn't reply, so I began to apologize, but he just kept saying it was good. I wasn't going to kiss his ass, so I left him out there. I don't even know how he got home, and I didn't give a   dam either.

When I got back up to the apartment, everyone was looking at me like I stole something.

"What y'all looking at me like that for?"

"You know it's gone be some shit now, right?" Hawk said.

Sammy said that Fame was shiest and vengeful, and if that's how he truly felt, he should have never been at the meeting in the first place. I ignored them and just walked away because I wasn't going to sit and listen to them take up for another NGHA.

The rest of the school year we didn't push anything. It was good too because if the heat was on us, it gave it time to cool out. The Noize Makers really didn't hang much. Everyone in the crew was doing they own thing.

I went back to Grand's house and began to get deeper into my poetry. Daja had me hooked, so most of my time was spent with her and Writing. She kept me grounded. Grand loved her so it was easy for us to spend time together because she could come over when she wanted.

Park Place and its activities were becoming a distant memory. The only thing that mattered was Poetry and Day-Day. I felt good because for a while I had my youth back. That was something I thought would never happen again.   I could tell that Grandma Rosa was happy I was home.

Daja and I were inseparable. She was my ace.   I wanted her to know it, so I went to the store and purchased a gold frame.   I then placed a picture that we took at military circle mall in it.   When I gave it to her she was excited.   I told her that she was right. Gold frames do last forever, and then she began to cry.   The fact that we were so young didn't matter to me.   I loved her and no one could tell me any different.   Daja and I were together every day until the end of the school year.

We spent a lot of time at Flipper's, the movies and my house.   I was happy, and it didn't take clothes or respect on the block to give it to me.   Like always, I knew it wouldn't last long.   The streets were calling me.

I thought about my mom a lot. Grand had a photo album full of her pictures. I looked like the male version of her minus the womanly features.   I don't know what made that time any different, but I was dying to see my mom.

For a long time I didn't want to talk t o her because of the letters I wrote that were left unanswered.   By this time I felt like I had nothing to lose because she was going to either write or not.   I wrote her almost every day, until the end of the school year without a reply.

I felt like she was treating me like I was dead, so I did the same, and didn't write her again.   In my life I don't regret much, but what I do regret was taking all of anger out on Daja.   I was bitter and you could see it on my face. My entire body language changed. It began to take a toll on us by the end of the school year because she said I was changing. As soon as love had come it was leaving, but I was so wrapped up in anger, nothing else mattered.

The final day of school had come and I was happy until Daja came over. She killed my whole vibe because she said she thought we needed some time. I was so pissed off that I put her out and told her to never come back. She left without a fight, and like my Mom, I felt like she didn't care. I think that's when I really started my bitterness towards women. My Grandma Rosa was the only one at that time who loved me unconditionally.

The summer had started with a bad omen. Daja's break up had me all out of wack. I wanted nothing more to do with her ever. I wanted to get my mind off of her. I need something fun to do and destiny answered. Hawk called and told us Big Bad Base and company were having an end of school jam. Base was another dude who had the party scene on lock for teens. He rented out the scope and was going to battle Bobby Roscoe. We knew it was going to be jumping, but one thing we also knew. It was going to be a gladiator's circle.

The summer jam was definitely going to pull all of the hoods in. We had to roll deep. We got all of our boys from Park Place and caught the bus. We were about 25 strong. At a dance like that one numbers meant everything. If you were caught with less than 10 you were in for a rough night.

We went in fly as usual. I rocked the red Lee Jeans with the red and white suede Pumas to match. A pair of all white Gazelles covered my eyes, and my head was adorned with a white and red Kangol. Nobody could match our jewels. We all had the Cuban link and a baby dope rope with "NOIZE" on the nameplate. Park Place was shinning. We knew other crews would be their representing their hood so we were on alert all night. We saw Diggs Park and Oak leaf together, which gave them some strong numbers because they untied neighborhoods. Curry Park was with Tidewater and Young Park. We saw Huntersville, Lindenwood Ballentine, Bowling Park, Marshall Manor and Roberts Park to name a few. We combined forces when we saw Divine walk in with his Lamberts Point crew. Divine had always been cool with me. We went to Blair together and he hung with us like we were crew. Most of the time, Lamberts Point and Park Place had beef but never Divine and I. He was one the cooler Point boys.

We were all chilling in the middle of the floor and all of a sudden "Throw that D," by "Two Live Crew" comes on and the crowd got open. Girls were on the floor throwing it in little miniskirts. Bobby Roscoe then comes with Perfect Beat by Soul Sonic force. I was on the dance floor riding this girl when a fly little shorty was giving me the eye from the corner. As I was dancing she was licking her tongue and laughing with her girls. She definitely had my attention. I stopped dancing and went over to her and asked for her name. She just laughed and I asked again. When she was about to tell me…it happened!

The first fight of the night broke out. We had been there for about two hours and I thought it would have been happened. The alliance between Oak leaf and Diggs Park went bad somewhere down the line and they started brawling against each other. All of Park Place and Lamberts Point got together and huddle with our backs against the wall. Sammy told me to look in the center of the floor and who did I see throwing it hard. It was Daja! I played it off well but I was lifted. I wanted to go and snatch her off the floor. I knew the best way to get at her was to do the same thing.

The fight was ended quickly by security and I saw the girl I was about to kick it to before it started. I went up and grabbed her by the hand and headed to the dance floor. I was grinding on her like I was trying to tare through her jeans. I knew it would catch Daja's attention. She looked over and started staring at us. She wasn't even dancing anymore. I rocked harder and even smirked while I was gripping my hands on her rump shaker. All of a sudden Daja ran over and popped shorty girl with a thunderous slap...dead in her dam mouth! Shorty went flying on the floor and all of Park Place's girls started wearing her A** out. I felt bad so I tried to break it up and some dude snuffed me in my jaw. The Noize makers went ballistic. He got me good too because everything I saw transpire was from floor's view. I was stumbling to my feet and I saw a hand reach out to me. It was Fame. He had blood on his shirtsleeve. He grabbed me up and as the fiasco was coming to an end I saw the floor empty and two people were laid out. We all got out of The Scope like runaway slaves. I thanked Fame once we got outside. I also apologized again for what had happened and we settled the beef between us. Fame was really Noize and he proved it that night

Instead of catching the bus we all walked home together. It was a crazy night. Daja and her girls walked with us but I didn't have too many words for her. She was the reason for all of the stupidity that night. She wanted to shine on me but when I shined back she couldn't take it. We got to Colonial Avenue and said peace to the Lamberts Point squad. They were definitely down with us that night despite our neighborhood beef. Sammy and the crew went to Aunt Marisa's but I wanted to go home. I really didn't I just wanted to walk with Daja but I didn't want to let her know that.

"Soooo...are you heading my way big guy?" She tried to say in a sexy voice.

"Not really, I'm going to Newport Ave."

"Why you trying to play me like what I did didn't turn you on Baker? It really did. I couldn't help but smirk. She grabbed me by the hand and we walked to her Grandfather's house. I sat with her on the porch and talked with her for about an hour. I knew the reason she wanted to break up was because summer had arrived...well I was playing out too. No one wanted to be in a relationship in the summer because that was when all the fun would happen.

"Does this mean we still single?

"I guess it doesn't Baker. I don't want anyone else to have you but me!" We kissed for about two minutes and said our goodbyes. I was kind of happy. I really loved Daja even though I knew she wasn't the one for me

The next morning would mark the start of us going to the big game. While sitting at the kitchen eating some Honeycomb cereal, my Grand came in with some news that changed the course of our life forever. She told me her brother Felipe wanted her to spend some time with the family in New York. By the end of the week, Grand, Sammy and I embarked on journey that would put us on Noize on the next level!

Baker Grimes
Hamza Atoi
CHAPTER FIVE

Once we arrived at JFK Airport, you could smell the difference between Virginia and the Big Apple. Things looked like they had sped up about 20 miles per hour more than the life we knew back home.

As we walked through the terminal we could hear a loud choppy accent in the distance. It was vulgar and rude. I was saying to my self

"These New Yorker's are as crazy as they say!"

And right after that thought the same voice screamed out my Abuela's name with excitement. It was her little brother Felipe. Grand use to tell us stories about her crazy little brother "Flip." We hadn't seen Uncle since we were very young and we were too young to remember how wild he truly was. One thing I do know, Uncle Flip loved his sister dearly and saw that she never ever wanted for anything. .

Later that night Uncle Flip had a big party in his Brown Stone on the Lower East Side. My Uncle was a big lover of Celia Cruz and her Azucar melodies filled the air along with other prominent Dominican artist. Grand also loved Soca. It was a Dominican tradition to dance with the elders when we all came together for reunions. Grand showed us all by grooving to Conga's played by Uncle Flip. She was very graceful for her age and enticed the eyes of even the young men present with her movements. For an older woman I have to say, my Grand put a lot of younger women to shame with her looks and figure.

While everyone was engulfed in the night's festivities, Sammy and I went on the front stoop and tried to blend into the Big City life. While we were sitting having the time of our life, a car pulled up with all my hopes and dreams inside the passenger seat. I stared because this was the day I prayed for, but as I looked closer all my hopes and dreams began to fade away.

"Mis primos," This beautiful voice screamed with delight.

It felt like I was staring for an eternity.

"Are going to stand there or are you going to hug my neck Baker?"

It was my cousin Celia who I hadn't seen since my mom was locked away. The strangest part of it all was the fact she was the spitting image of my mother. She had the same build, hair color, eye color, voice, and look. I couldn't believe how much they looked alike. It was as if she were my mom's twin sister.

"I know Bake; I look just like Auntie right?"

I was still stunned.

"Bake!" Sammy said with an aggravated tone.

"Man snap out of it!"

I then put the biggest smile on my face and hugged her neck like she was mother.

She was rolling with this tall dark skinned dude with a walk like he was Eddie Murphy's comedic character "Dexter Saint Jock." I knew by his swagger he was Jamaican even before he opened his mouth.

"Blessed likkle yout!"

I didn't crack a smile at him. It was something about him I didn't like straight from the beginning and I had always been a very good judge of bull crap. I didn't speak. I just looked back at Celia and shot her a look like... really! Sammy nudged me and went to shake hands with him.

"Peace My name's Sammy, the rude one over there is Bake. He just little over protective over family but he cool."

"Cool, Mi name Cutta."

Cutta and I kept extreme eye contact while we all conversed. His smile had gone from grin to smirk. Yeah I had him. The eyes never lie and he wasn't one to be trusted at all. Let Sammy tell it, I didn't trust anyone anyway

Uncle Flips Brown Stone had a basement that Celia and her sister Cinda called home. It was dope as ever. It looked like it was separate from Uncle Flip's Crib. They had it laid out. Celia had this huge king type chair and it was plush. I went to sit down and Cutta beat me to it.

"Dis here be mine Likkle Yout." He said with a sadistic tone. I just stared at him. All of a sudden I felt a smack at the back of my head. Celia had popped the hell out of me.

"What was that for?'

She said with the sweetest voice ever uttered.

"We don't do things like that in our Familia Primo, You know better."

She was right because if Grand were standing there she would have done the same thing. I went up to Cutta and apologized even though I kept the same feelings about him as I had before. It was cool. I just kept my feelings on the low and watched him without it being so obvious.

Before we noticed, it was about 5 in the morning.

Time had flown from the time of being picked at the airport until then. I was tired as a two year old without a nap. Celia looked in my eyes and like my mother use to instinctively do. She knew I was tired. She set up a pallet for Sammy and I and I crashed hard without even saying goodnight. Before my eyes closed I was blessed with the last look of Celia tucking me in just like my mom use to do when I was young.

I awoke in the morning to the smell of eggs bacon and fresh Orange juice. Celia was in the kitchen cooking just like Grand and Mommy use to do. It felt just like home there. Inside that Brownstone it felt like home. Sammy and I got up and we readied ourselves for breakfast. I was in a good mood until I saw Cutta come out of Celia's room in his boxers and Wife Beater. I had a chance to take a good look at him. I wanted his image burned in my mind because He was real shady looking to me. I was taught at a young gage to pay attention to everything and remember it all.

Cutta had a slim tall build. He looked like was about 6'4 and had locks that were about as tall as he. His mouth was full of gold teeth and his chest looked like he had definitely been in a war a time or two.

"Hey Cutta! What happen to your chest?"

Cutta looked down at his chest and then looked at me and said "War likkle Yout...War."

He begins to tell me about his life back in Jamaica. He was from a place called "Jungle." With no more smile present he begin to tell me tales of famine and murder. His oldest brother was murdered over a deal gone badly. Cutta's mom also died in a hail of gunshots because of the retaliation Cutta's crew took after his brother's death. He said after that he took his little brother "Fire" and his little sister "Queen" to the airport and flew them to the states to live with an aunt until he arrived two years later. He continued to tell his story over breakfast. Sammy and I listened intently. We were glued to his every word. After he finished I felt like I should ease up on him.

After breakfast we showered and put on our clothes because Celia and Cutta were going to take us shopping. I was oh, so ready to hit the New York Malls because my homeboy "Boogiemonster" from Brooklyn use to have the dope gear. He had garments that didn't hit V.A. until months later, and was the first one I saw on that Dapper Dan SHT.

We ran upstairs and kissed Grand, gave Uncle Flip a pound and we were out. Grand just smiled because she knew how excited we were.

Cutta had a sweet ride. It was a Jeep Cherokee with KC lights on the top. It was money green and gold. It was dope! Sammy and I stared out the window as we drove all around the big city.

"Wait till you see it at night my yout, it is very dope as you youngsters say."

Cutta was starting to grow on me. I loved the way he treated my cousin too. He often smiled at her even when she wasn't looking and to me that showed a sign of love and loyalty.

Hey Cut! I heard a lot about Queens when you gone show us your hood!"

I was excited. We had shopped all day and we didn't even spend any of our money because Celia and Cutta bought us everything. I know they had to spend at least a G-stack on both of us. Then my mind started wondering. Where was he getting all of this money? Well it didn't take a rocket scientist but sometimes assumptions will make an, well you know the phrase. We stopped on Linden Boulevard at this banging Caribbean joint called the "Golden Krust." The food was hitting. I ordered a large Ox Tails with red beans and rice plus a side of coco bread and plantain. I stuffed my face until I was sinfully fulfilled. By that time it was getting dark and I definitely wanted to see what N.Y. looked like when the sun left the city. We all stay and versed with each other until the sun gave up its position and let the moon handle things for a while.

We took a ride to Mid-Town Manhattan and I was amazed. Celia kept telling me not to look up but I couldn't. It was like clans of illuminating giants were hovering over us.

"Hey Primo! You are going to look like a tourist if you keep that up, blend in with your surroundings, and don't let it get you."

I understood what she was saying but I was already entranced by the magic of the cities lights. I eventually snapped out of it but it is a memory that I hold dear to myself. I loved New York and still do!

It was getting late and about time for us to head home but Cutta needed to make a stop first. We drove up to 149th and Amsterdam then Cutta's entire mood changed. It was like he was a different person. He jumped out of his jeep and approached a group of dudes dressed fresher than Dougie and the Get Fresh crew. They all gave each other this peculiar handshake. Cutta then moved through the group toward this one guy in the back who was shaking like a stripper. He just stared at this guy for about a minute and then he looked at one of his obvious goons and shook his head. Boom, one shot and the dude dropped like a bag of groceries. Two of his crew pick up the body and tossed him in a trashcan on the street. Cutta walked away unshaken. He jumped back in the Jeep and we drove off like nothing had ever happened. Sammy and I didn't look surprised. We act like what just transpired didn't. Celia just looked forward the whole time and didn't make a sound.

"Every ting good likkle yout?"

We straight, you alright homie?" Sammy said in a way of letting him know we weren't afraid of what just happened.

"I just want to make sure we don't have any problems."

Of course I answered with a hot head.

"That's your problem not ours, we can careless about what we didn't see. Do you feel me?"

Cutta just smiled. He didn't know death was something we had already seen and unfortunately been a part of.

We got back to Uncle Flip's at about Midnight. As I was getting out of the car, Cutta grabbed my hand.
"Eyes that see sometimes don't!" I answered with my own brand sarcasm.
"And hands that grab sometimes disappear!"
I knew what he meant by the entire statement and I wanted him to know that I was not moved by his words. He looked at Celia and she tried to discreetly shake her head at him. He let me go and Sammy put his razor back in his mouth. Cutta must have caught a glimpse of what happen and instantly knew we weren't average kids. He just looked at Sammy, smiled and then drove off.

We never talked about what went on that night to Celia. We just moved on like it never happened. Sammy and I on the other hand knew we were dealing with a real methodical dude and we wanted to know what his angle was.

We had been in New York for about week and all we did was shop. It was getting boring. How much money could we spend and how much clothes could we buy without any one seeing how we got down. We wanted go somewhere and be seen. We wanted to show out a little.

Cutta told us of this skate party they were having in Harlem. He told us his little brother and sister was going and wanted to know if we wanted to roll also. We were surely with it. I was ready to shine and show off the new gear and jewelry I had just coped. Sammy and I were ready! I put on my Adidas and Adidas track suit. We both also threw on our Eric B and Rakia dope ropes with the two-inch pinky rings with "NOIZE" inscribed.

Cutta picked us up at about 7PM in a Black Volvo with Fendi seats. I have to say, the way those New York boys use to hook up their cars was the Jank! In the front seat was the most beautiful girl I had ever seen. I mean… she was way more banging in the face than Daja. She looked like an Egyptian Queen. I could tell it was Cutta's little brother sitting the back because Cutta and he looked just a like. Celia gave us a kiss and told us to be careful and keep our eyes open at all times because we weren't in VA. Sammy and I got in the back with Cutta's little brother. We all instantly hit off. Fire was the coolest. He was actually just like us. We had the same style, mannerisms and killer instinct. Queen was a little more reserved. She didn't talk much but she did laugh at parts of our conversation

We got to skating ring and jumped out of the car like celebrities. Everyone knew who Fire and Queen were and we rode the wave of popularity with them. The line was long as hell and we just walked in like it wasn't there. We didn't even pay. You could see the haters being fueled with by our VIP status but who cared. I kept my swagger on billionaire boys' club level.

Once inside it was on. All I saw was a pool of girls on skates under flashing lights. Sammy, Fire and I just smiled because we were about to embark on a booty parade and we were the host of ceremonies. Queen slid off to the side to a group of girls who look like Salt and Pepper. They were the epitome of dope.

New York girls had a fly girl style. It kind of reminded me of the girls back home in Norfolk.

Skating wasn't either Sammy's or my thing so we just hung on the side with Fire. We also knew getting caught on skates wasn't a good idea for us because if someone was ready to fight you didn't have time to take them off. We just profiled and conversed with every girl that walked passed us. We were like magnets because everyone wanted to be where we were. Sammy, Fire and I stayed surrounded by girls dipped in fly mini-skirts and tight Sassoon Jeans, bamboo earrings, asymmetrical and doobies hairstyles. You would have thought LL Cool J was in the building by the way they flocked us.

As the night progressed I saw the plumpest rump I had ever seen on a girl. She had some tight Jordache jeans with some ruffled socks coming out of her illuminated skates. As she made her revolutions around the ring, she would wink her eye at me. She knew how to get a man's attention and I knew how to except it. I motioned to her to come over and she glided to me like she was ready for action.

"I see you looking shorty, what's your name?"

She giggled, "Oshun."

"Where are you from you sound country?"

"Country, I'm not from the country I'm from Virginia!"

"Yeah you are country, my brother Big Dog use to take us there. You ever heard of Va. Beach?"

"Of course, I live about 17 miles from there; the strip is where we hang at in the summer."

"So, what brings you here with your fine country A**?"

"We're visiting some relatives."

I see your money isn't as short as you!"

"Neither is monster but we can talk about him when we get more aquatinted." She knew where I was coming from.

"I love monsters maybe I can star him in my new horror movie?" She was ready and willing but I played my cards like I wasn't sweating her even though I wasn't going to let that bubble get away from me for no reason!

I gave her the number to Uncle Flips Crib and to Grand's house back in Virginia. As I was getting her number I had to piss real bad.

"I'll be right back shorty."

I ran to the bathroom quick because those five flavor sodas were on my trail. When I got inside I yanked out my monster as a sigh of relief came over me, the door creaked. I looked over my shoulder and three dudes where standing at the door looking at me. I got into think mode because I knew this was about to be something bad.

"What up Son, those jewels look fresh B, let me hold one?"

I didn't respond, I was ready to react because my hands where real nice. I had been boxing since I was 6 years old and the training gave me a body chiseled by God himself. I wanted them to test me. Then the odds changed. The loud mouth dude pulled out a small chrome 25-caliber pistol. There wasn't anything my hands could do with that so I stepped back. As they began to approach, this big black scary dude walked in. I knew I was done.

"We got a problem?"

"No we don't have any problems." I said with a calm shaky voice.

"I wasn't talking to you I'm talking to these little gods right here."

I looked down and he was holding a snug nose 357 Magnum at the back of one the three.

Oh snap! What up Hush! We don't have any problems B!"

They dashed out of the bathroom like they had seen a ghost.

"Don't get caught with your pants down god!" He then motioned for me to follow him out. Fire and Sammy saw the three guys run out of the bathroom and ran over to the restroom with a small mob. The big guy looked at them all as they parted like the red sea.

"You good primo?"

"Yeah I'm straight."

"Who was that?"

"I don't know but he definitely looked out!"

Fire told us "Hush" was one of his brother's old bodyguards. He said they had some beef and he lost his job and his right eye. Hush had this huge Buck fifty down his face and his right eye was a gray color from the obvious battle wound. Queen rushed over and shoved all of us towards the door. Once we got outside Celia and Cutta were waiting with an entourage of goons.

"Primo you ok?"

Yeah I'm fine, what's all this for? It was just some dudes trying to get some shine, it's all good."

Cutta got a call from Queen saying she saw Hush follow me in the bathroom and in their eyes that was bad news about to be delivered. As we jumped in the car to leave, Hush came walking out and just stood looking in our direction. Celia Immediately got in the car and so did Cutta. While driving away Hush nodded his head at me and I nodded back in appreciation with a smile. Man, New York gave me its first taste of hood life first hand.

We got back to Uncle Flips and went down to Celia and Cinda's Basement apartment. Celia sat down in her plush fur recliner and gave a big sigh of relief. She just looked at me and smiled like she was glad I was ok. I guess in my eyes, I didn't know the severity of the matter, but how could I the dude saved me!

I asked Celia what was the beef with Cutta and Hush and all she would tell me was Hush was unpredictable. I then told her what happened but she wasn't enthused. I left it all alone and begin to talk to Sammy about Oshun.

"Yo Sammy I met this Phat little jank at the ring tonight."

"I saw her!" She was thicker than cold grits Bake!"

We were having a great time In New York but we knew destiny was a trickster and wanted her fun also! One Saturday morning Celia and Cutta decided to take us to the mall to shop but we had other plans. Cutta had no problem dropping Grand money on us so we thought it was time for little southern hospitality. Sammy and I decided to treat them to a nice day out. We hit this well known Jewelry spot in Manhattan and had them make a 14kt set of bamboo earrings with Celia's name inside, and got Cutta a two inch pinky ring with "Untouchable" engraved. It cost us a pretty penny but we wanted to show them how we got down. We had a small bag full of money with us that only Sammy and I knew about. We knew we were going to floss plus we wanted to bring the Noize Makers back something from the city. After shopping we took them Uptown to eat

Cutta had this real amazed look on his face because he knew we had spent real dough on them that day. While we were eating both of them were just looking at us crazy in the face.

Sammy just smiled and said, "Yeah homie you not the only one who get money! What you thought Benjamin's stopped when they met you?"

We all had a good time during dinner that night, and we really enjoyed the time we had with Cutta. He showed us all of New York, and introduced us to his squad as his "little moneymakers." He had this twinkle in his eye as we rode around the city meeting all of the major players. He had something in the works for us. It was written all over his smile.

Baker Grimes
Hamza Atoi

CHAPTER SIX

I think the highlight of the entire New York trip was Queen. Let me tell you homie. She was the dopiest female I had ever encountered. When I first saw her I tried not to look but she caught me and gave me the prettiest smirk.

Queen was more than an around the way girl. She had mad swagger too. She wasn't like all the other New York a chick I ran into in my short time there. Queen was unique. She was a sophomore in high school, and attended Fiorella H. LaGuardia High School for the performing arts. You know that high school homie? It was the Famous "Fame" school. She played classical piano and could sing jazz like she was Lena Horne or Ella Fitzgerald. She had a love for poetry also, so you know that had me hype.

I remember reading Celia a couple of my pieces one day and she thought it would be a good idea if we all went to the Nuyorican Café. It was this well-known poetry and theater spot in the lower eastside of Brooklyn. All of the major poets from around the country had performed there and one of my favorites was co-founder "Miguel Pinero." Pinero had always been one my favorite poet because of his true to life poems. I studied Walt Whitman, Lord Alfred Tennyson, Robert Frost, Langston Hughes and Paul Roberson, but I really couldn't relate. Pinero was right up my alley. He spoke about addictions, poverty and real hood problems. There were a couple other poets who I came to love later in life like Talaam Acey, Narubi Selah, Lamar Hill, Will "Da Real One" Bell and 13 of Nazareth. I only wished one day I could be on their level because they spit fire! I feared it wasn't in the cards because dudes like me. I wanted to grace stages like them but a pen and pad wasn't high priority when your main responsibility is feeding the block its medicine.

Celia Called Queen to come along because of her love for the arts as well. I dressed down that night because in the poetry realm you could be ordinary. It wasn't about the gear or the jewels. All you needed was a notebook and an open mind.

When we picked up Queen she was dressed like her name. She had on this beautiful African type shirt and her hair was wrapped like an Egyptian goddess. She smelled like fresh cut jasmine and her smile lit up the dark, smog filled street. Queen would always greet you with the word "Peace." She was very soft spoken. I loved her voice. Her dark chocolate skin, pearl white teeth and heaven like smile had me from the first day I saw her. I knew I couldn't run game on a girl like that.

"Peace all." She got in the car hips swinging into the seat as if they were trying to entice me to look. I did!

"So how do you like New York so far King?"

"You talking to me?"

"I don't see any other fine guy in the car."

I was hooked! I just smiled and so did Celia. Celia had it set up all along because she knew Queen thought I was good looking.

I settled down and Queen and I had the most interesting first conversation since Daja. It was like the ride through Brooklyn had love theme music to it. I felt like I was in a movie. Queen was what I needed.

We got to the Nuyorican cafe and it was packed. People were sitting everywhere. They had drummers and beating tribal tunes as poets evoked their deepest emotions and shared them with the crowd. Queen and I sat side by side hand in hand as words entered our ears capturing our attention. All of a sudden the host got up and said they had a special guest and called me up. I was shook. I looked at Celia and stared at Queen. I didn't put my name on the list so why was he calling me? Celia knew the host and signed me up on the list without me knowing. The crowd applauded awaiting my arrival to the stage but I was frozen. I had never read any of my work for anyone but Celia and Sammy. I didn't want to go up. "Celia I can't!"

"Yes you can Primo, read the piece I like called She. Trust me they are going to love it."

I looked over at Queen and she had positioned herself in a manner that said to me she was ready to hear my work. Her movement was so sexy I couldn't possibly keep her in suspense any longer. I stepped to the stage slow. It felt like I was walking forever. When I got to the mic. The crowd grew silent. I didn't introduce myself I just recited it. As I read my eyes were stuck on Queen as if I was reading the poem to

her in a secluded room with just her and I. Her eyes held on to every word. She licked her lips as if she could taste my poem. When I finished, the crowd went bonkers. I almost ran off the stage. The host was this beautiful Puerto Rican sister and she said to the crowd,
"When he grows up ladies, don't even bother because he is mine!" I felt good. Queen hugged me and gave me a big kiss on my cheek and held my arm like I was hers.

The night of poetry had come to an end. On the way home all queen could do was stare at me. She wasn't even saying anything. When we got to her home she asked was I going to call her and I told I didn't have her number.
"Yes you do silly, look in your right pocket." Somewhere in the night's adventure, Queen had slipped me her number.
"I really enjoyed you tonight Baker, Peace till next time my King."

She swung her hips out of the car the same way she swung them in. I couldn't wait to call. On the way home Celia and I just laughed and recanted the night of fun. My New York trip was coming to an end and after that night I wanted it to last an eternity.

When I got her home, the house looked vacant. It was about 1am and no one was home. This was odd to Celia so she went into the main part of the brownstone where Uncle Flip resided and no one was home. She came back out and we went into her basement apartment and found Cinda there crying.

"Cinda what's wrong honey?" Cinda couldn't stop crying.

"Sammy has been shot!" I fell to my knees. Even though Sammy was my cousin, he was also my best friend. If anything had happen to him New York was going to see a side of me that was horrific.

"Where are they?" I screamed! She told us they were at a hospital in Queens. Cinda said she was waiting for us to get home. I asked her what happen and she said Fire and Sammy went out with Asia and Oshun. They went to some party in Queens and Sammy and Fire was shot after a brawl took place. The bad news didn't stop there she said Fire was dead. Celia dropped like a bag of potatoes. Fire was like her little brother and they were very close. I had hell in my eyes. I wanted to vengeance and was going to get it!

We got to the Hospital and Grand, Uncle Flip and two of uncles boys were there.

"Granny what happen?" Grand was just silent. No tears and no words. I knew she was praying I just let her be. I paced the hospital floors planning an assault in my mind. I had every intention to find out what happen so I could kill all involved. My thoughts were very sinister and that was the day I knew I had a peculiar thirst for blood.

I re-played the razor-cutting incident back in Virginia over and over in my head. I was ready to go further.

I never had any remorse for either confrontation. I felt very numb after both and slept very well after those nights. As those bizarre thoughts were taking over my thought process, a doctor came out of the room and headed straight to grand.

"Your grandson sustained a serious gunshot wound to his chest. He lost quite a bit of blood but he is stable and will survive."

Grand just looked towards the heavens and smiled. I was relieved. The doctor said he was in recovery and we couldn't see him until the morning. Grand said it was no reason to stay at the hospital and said it would be a good idea if we went home. I didn't want to leave and she knew I didn't so she allowed me to stay with Celia and Cinda.

"I know you little Santo. Don't let thoughts consume you ok, Sammy will be fine." She kissed me on my cheek and her and Uncle Flip left. I overheard Celia talking to Cinda about what they heard happen. My question was this. When did Sammy talk to Asia and Oshun about going anywhere? Sammy normally told me everything and he never once mentioned he and Fire going to some party, let alone with Asia and Oshun. I couldn't figure it out. Out of nowhere Cutta came into the waiting room they had set up for us. He had hell in his eyes. Celia hugged him and as she was hugging him he looked at me. It was a look like I had something to do with it all. I stared him back in his face because I was going to be stared down. He had picked the wrong time to FCK with me.

"Where that likkle white liver Baker?

"Why in the hell would I know?"

He continued to look at me like I was suspect. I had no time for his bull so I called him out.

"Look I know your brothers gone and I'm sorry, but if you keep looking at me like you want something I'm gone give it to you!"

He couldn't understand I was hurt also. Fire was a new friend but it was like he was family. My whole entire trip had been spent with Him, Cutta and Celia. Why would I cross him and what made him think that way?

Time must have been on some Nascar SHT because it flew by in old the turmoil. The Doctors said Sammy was alert and we all could go inside and see him. I went in his room and you could tell he was a little groggy from the surgery. His eyes were weak but I could see his strength in his heart.

"I know what you think Primo, and we gone handle this once I get right!" He said with a mellow tone. Is fire Ok, he asked? We all just stared. He didn't know.

"Where is Fire?" he asked again. He said the last he remembered was Asia and Oshun backing up and then gunshots. He said as he was falling he saw Fire run for him and then everything went black. What was most interesting, he said Hush had come to him earlier that night and tried to give him a bulletproof vest. He said he didn't want because it was too bulky and would have made his gear look busted. He said Hush also was trying to warn him about something but he was so into Asia he didn't hear a word Hush was saying.

"So where is Fire? Why the FCK y'all just standing there like you don't understand what I'm saying?"

"He's gwan star!" Cutta said with tears building in his eyes.

"What you mean he gone!"

"He was shot in the head and found in an alley." Celia added with a sad tone. Now the story had taken a chilling turn. Sammy was shot at the party but Fire was shot and found in an alley? Sammy Said he saw Fire run toward him when the shots rang out, so why was Fire found away from the party? I couldn't figure it out. I called Oshun but no one answered her phone. I wanted to break the ice between Cutta and I so I told him I was down for whatever if he had a plan. He looked at me and apologized and so did I. I knew he was just upset and was lashing out because I knew Oshun. His pager went off and he said he had to go but he would contact us later. He told Sammy he was going to get him an ill tattoo to cover up his scare, smiled and left. Something was about to go down I could feel it.

A couple days went by and Sammy was able to leave the hospital. He had minor pain and was really getting along well for a boy who had just been shot but his eyes were different. When we were at Celia's he often stared into the distance and said nothing. He didn't even want to play Tecmo Bowl. I remember him recanting the story and he said hush told him to watch Cutta. He said he paid it no mind because to him Cutta was cool. He also said he remembered two of Cutta's boys staring him down the whole night but he didn't think anything of it. He thought they were there for him. What didn't play out right to him was the fact Asia and Oshun called him out of the blue and said they wanted a half brick did they know anyone they could cop one from. Now the story was starting to come together. He said he called Cutta and Cutta's boys dropped it off to him and Fire. He said they then went to the party to meet them and do the deal there.

Now the puzzle had more of what I needed to try and figure it out. I asked Sammy why did he go without me and he said Oshun didn't want me to come because she was interested in Fire and she didn't want to hurt my feelings. She said after the deal they were going to party and he could talk with Asia, which they did. Sammy said he was going to tell me but I was already gone with Celia when it all went down. I asked him how did he get there and he said Cutta dropped Fire and him off.

Why would Cutta act like he didn't know anything? He came in the hospital questioning me like he didn't have a clue what could have just happen.

I asked Sammy did they sell the work. He said yes and Fire was holding on to the money.

"It was a set up Bake! I ain't stupid. That BTCH set us up!"

I agreed with him but it had to go larger than those two. Cutta's two boys were in my mind and the fact they were gritting on my primo didn't sit light with me. I also wanted to know why Hush was trying to save us so much. What interest in our survival did he have?

The summer was over and we were three days from being on a plane back to Virginia. I was happy in a way but I really wanted to resolve what happen to my Sammy before I left. Destiny heard my cries for vengeance and gave me an opportunity for blood.

Cutta came over while we were packing. It was about 3pm and asked if I wanted to see Queen before I left. I was with it. He told Sammy we would be back he was going to let me spend some alone time with queen then he was going to come back and take Sammy shopping before we left. Sammy declined the offer, which was crazy. He loved shopping more than females. I paid it no mind. All I had on my brain was Queen.

We drove down New York Avenue far away from where they lived and my spider senses went up.

"Where we going Cutta?"

He said he had two dudes I wanted to talk to and they had info on what happen to Sammy and Fire. I didn't know what he was talking about and I never asked him about no one. What was he planning? I had my Nine on me I got from Uncle Flips arsenal at his house, so if things got too funny looking I was going to shoot my way out and do my best to find my way back to Uncle Flip's. We stopped at this abandoned looking apartment and he said to me "let's go." I just sat there and I was ready to fire off because it didn't look right.

"You're a smart yout' Baker that's why mi a deal wit' you rude boy, but mi no here to romp with you. Two of my crew are in there duck taped pon' a chair ready to answer questions."

I still was hesitant but if it was my time, I wasn't going to go alone and destiny was going to make sure of that.

Once inside I saw a gruesome scene. Cutta's boys were bloodied up near death. Cutta had five of his other crew inside and they had two Pit bulls with blood salivating front their mouths. He handed me a machete and said if they don't answer right I could convinced them. I had another thought in mind, so I approached one Cutta's ex henchman and I slit his throat. The room was in shock. Cutta asked what was I doing and I told him if the other one didn't want to speak he could get the same thing but slower. He started singing like a canary. He said Asia called him up and told him about a sting they could stage to get money. He wasn't happy with Cutta and said Cutta wasn't feeding him like he thought he should be fed. After I got all the info I needed I told him I was lying. I duct taped his mouth and chopped off his hands and watched him bleed all over the plastic set up on the floor. Cutta and his crew just stared at me.

"Let's get you out of here Bake and set up stage two. Are you down?"

I was down. I didn't want to leave New York without revenge and I was getting my wish.

Cutta said he knew where Asia was and we needed to hit her next. He had it all planned out because he knew I was about to leave and no one really knew me so it would be easy to disappear after it all took place.

I was as hungry as a hippo in a children's board game so I asked Cutta if we could stop and get something to eat. It was now approaching dusk. We went to one his spots in Brooklyn and whom did we happen to see hugged up on some a dude in a parked car? It was Asia. My appetite diminished quickly.

"Hey Cut! You see what I see?"

What's up Grimy?"

I told him look across the street. He looked and saw the same thing my eyes were locked on. I jumped up without waiting for him and walked slowly across the street then fired my whole clip into the car. Cutta dashed out of the restaurant and pulled me away from the scene and we were out.

"RASS! Why you not wait for me?"

I saw an opportunity and I took it. When I left out of the restaurant it wasn't on a dummy move. Before we went in I already knew how I was going to do it. I was smart with my choices and was ready to deal with the consequences also. On the way out Cutta just smiled and told me I was a crazy little boy.

"I need more of you on my team seen!" However I didn't do it for him. I did it because my family was all I had and if you touched any part of it, it was with a price!

I got back to Uncle Flip's and Cutta left after dropping me off. He didn't say anything he just smirked and drove off. When I got inside Sammy was playing Tecmo Bowl so I picked up the controller and told him reset it so we could play a game. He reset the game and stared at me. He just shook his head because the look I had in my eye he knew well. He didn't ask me anything he just told me he loved me and I told him the same and we preceded to whip each other in the video game we loved also.

I awoke the next morning to the smell of jasmine by my pillow. I rolled over and saw beauty wrapped under the blankets with me. It was Queen. She came over to spend my last day in New York with me.

"Peace my King!"

"Peace Queen, my love goes out to you and Cutta for your lost."

You could tell it was bothering her. After the funeral she didn't say anything. She didn't even cry. She told me as we lay there she had seen so much death in her family she was becoming numb. It wouldn't surprise her if Cutta would end up next the way her family tradition was going. She told me she loved her brother but he was real shady and would do anything for money. It didn't surprise me. I always had an ill feeling towards Cutta but I just couldn't figure out what it was.

It was like Queen was in a therapy session lying there with me. She told me about Cutta's relationship with Fire. It wasn't the brotherly love type relationship because he felt Fire was soft. He wanted Fire to be more like him. He wanted Fire to be a rude boy, but Fire didn't have Cutta's killer instinct in him. Fire was all about the ladies Queen said and to Cutta that made him vulnerable.

I listened to Queen release all she knew about her brother and it was information I needed to keep in my back pocket if anything ever jumped off between us. Cutta was very ruthless and had no loyalty. In her heart he was the reason they had to leave Jamaica. She felt like Cutta was the one behind her older brother's death. She heard rumors he was jealous of her older brother "Stinger" whom was one of the major rude boys in Jungle. The rumor was Cutta had Stinger go to a Pasa Pasa party and when Stinger was leaving he had his own crew murder Stinger and two of his bodyguards in front of everyone. When their mother was murdered, it was also rumored; that Cutta's crew did the deed so the truth wouldn't get back to Stinger's crew. They said their mother had first hand information Cutta was behind the hit. I couldn't believe what I was hearing. I saw how Queen acted around Cutta but I thought it was just a respect thing. She was very timid. If Cutta was this no remorse killer his legend claimed him to be, I didn't want him anywhere around my family.

I turned the mood around by asking her if she really liked my poem. She smiled and told me it was sexy! We both grinned and turned away from the depressing conversation. Out of the blue she kissed me. Her hand caressed my head as her other hand guided me towards her breast. I said to myself,

"No! Is this really about to happen?" It did. Queen allowed me to venture where no one had ever venture before. Well to keep it real it was my first time also so we were able to share a most special moment. It was like heaven visited me. I was sprung.

I didn't want to leave New York, but it was time to say our good-byes and head back to Norfolk.

Baker Grimes
Hamza Atoi
CHAPTER SEVEN

Once we got off the plane at Norfolk International Airport I could smell the difference between the New York air and ours. It was good to inhale the beauty of trees instead of trash and smog. I was going to miss that beautiful peculiar smell but Virginia was definitely missed. I wanted to see the crew and I also wanted to see Daja.

The Noize Makers got together the weekend we got back. They told us Swampman's case had taken a turn for the worst. Every other week he was in some type of fight in Norfolk Detention. We couldn't see him because we were minors and his mom was so far gone on crack she probably didn't know where he was. His trial had come to an end and he was convicted of third degree murder and sentenced to juvenile life. He wasn't going to get out until he was 21 years old and was waiting to be transferred to another facility.

Do-Wop and Big Sippi were locked without bail. We heard from some of his crew he wasn't getting out anytime soon and Do-Wop was in the infirmary. He got into some beef with another inmate and apparently he was a made-man inside. He was found bleeding to death in the shower from multiple slash wounds on his face and body.

Things were getting to be mad different. I came back from New York thinking I would get back to some kind of normal. I guess normal knew destiny and didn't want to mess with what she had in store for us because what happened next changed our lives forever.

I don't want to make this story too long so let me fast forward some and get to the good parts. Remember the dude Cutta? Well we got a call from Celia saying he wanted to hook us up because he heard about Do-Wop and Big Sippi. He said he could link us up with some work. I never knew until later how he knew our situation but that's what makes this story unique. It's also what made Cutta very intelligent. I never took him as a regular hustler but the steps he took to get us back on board put him on a Scarface level.

The deal went down easy. We stopped selling on the block and were now actually handling large amounts of product ourselves. We were trained and ready for war if anyone ever tried to take ours. We use to hit this warehouse that had a gun range in it on the regular. We were taught hand-to-hand combat by this dude who had been in the prison system and learned this skill called "52 blocks." We were becoming more than just kid dealers. We were becoming a crew that was more deadly than a lot of adults. We knew how to set up plots and how to maneuver if we saw a hit coming. We knew what to look for and what to do to end it quickly. Fame stayed on and took Swampman's spot. It was cool because Fame and I were starting to become crew for real.

Our money was growing up as quick as we were. I swear at an early age we were pushing at least four bricks a week by ourselves easily. Only time Cutta's men came around was to collect the dough and drop off the product and directions to the next locality. The four bricks we were pushing were turned into six and we had new clientele from some old connects we held through Big Sippi. No one ever tried us. Cutta's name was to synonymous with death. If they did try they were going to get a rude awakening because we were now trained killers.

It was getting real hard hiding all the money we were making.

We were handling too much weight for kids. We had to let Aunt Marisa get in on the deal as our accountant. She was always good with money. She opened an account for us overseas. She taught us how to stash cash in different areas around town just in case we had to make a mad dash away from Virginia. Aunt Marisa was now our liaison. She was the godmother of all our operations and it definitely wouldn't have been successful without her.

Cutta was happy with the move he made with us. It was Sammy I was concerned about. He really didn't like Cutta anymore and I couldn't figure it out. Aunt Marisa told me Sammy talked to her and he was making moves for the Noize Makers to eventually sever ties with Cutta. Sammy was talking crazy. All the work we were pushing undetected for Cutta wasn't going to ever be able to be severed. Cutta wasn't going to see that type of money go out the door because we wanted to set up shop for ourselves.

I tried to talk to him about it from time to time but he never would talk straight with me.

Money was flowing like Rakim. We were getting paid in full. Aunt Marisa even bought a new house out in Virginia Beach. We kept the apartment out Park Place as a front but we were on the move. We controlled all of the dope that was moving through Park Place and half of Norfolk without anyone knowing it was us. They all thought Aunt Marisa was taking over for Mr. Maurice.

Time was moving by quickly and were all in high school. Maury High wasn't going to be anything new for me because everyone already knew me. I wasn't on Daja's mind but of course when I got there she was on her jealousy game. She was turning into a certified gold digger and girls like that were bad for business so I stayed my distance. We had a lot to lose from that point. This is no joke when I tell you this. I was only fifteen at that time and we were making about 10 grand a week. We were paid. We had every style you could imagine and even the ones that had not come out yet.

Dealing with Daja was starting to be a pain in the backside. She was always in my face trying to insinuate we were together. I really didn't have any love for her because I was truly sprung over Queen. I had no one else on my mind. I would talk to her often and visit during school breaks. Daja however wouldn't let up. She was on a mission and I was the goal. Why she wanted me so bad wasn't a mystery. I was the man and had dough.

I remember we were at one of our High School football games. It was Maury versus Lake Taylor. Lake Taylor was a moneymaking school and had a lot of little hustlers that were getting paid but not on our level. A lot of Oak Leaf Park boys held it down along with their rivals Diggs Park. The whole crew was in attendance like always minus Swampman who was still locked. Fame was the new member and had now become certified NOIZE. We all were flyer than two kites on a windy day at Mount Trashmore.

We dressed in unison but just different colors. Jean shorts with a polo shirt and Diadoras on our feet. When we walked in the gate you could feel all eyes on us. We played them at Norview High. It was across the streets from this area notorious for handling outsiders called "Wellington Oaks." I remember they left these dudes from Boston in a Benz dead but looking like they were lounging. They were big on the murder game out there!

Everyone wanted to be by us. Chicks were coming down from the other end and our plan to be ordinary was over. Our gear alone let everyone know we were somebody.

We were sitting down watching our school dismantle Lake Taylor. Man Maury was deep in talent that year. We really didn't go for the game though. We went to be seen. The star power was going to our head and we didn't even recognize it. I guess we wouldn't have. In spite of it all were just kids.

The night was going well. I was grabbing numbers like I was working for Harlem's Bumpy Johnson. I was getting one number and heard a voice that was still sexy as ever to me.

"So I guess my number isn't the number one anymore?"

It was Daja. She was with her little diva crew. I have to say Daja was fly. She was an around the way chick. She had on some bamboo earrings a body suit with rider boots, and the herringbone I bought her.

"That chain looks familiar shorty." She smiled and I was starting to get drawn in. Feelings were starting to re-emerge even though I knew she wasn't good for business and I.

Sammy gave this look but I ignored it. He knew me well. I had all these girls to pick from and now Daja was back on the scene and made me forget all of the numbers I just grabbed. She asked me what I was going to do with all of the digits I acquired and I just looked at her and smiled. I pulled the numbers from my pocket, ripped them up and said, "What numbers?" She had me once again. I didn't see it as a bad thing but bad was on its way for sure.

Sammy had his license and bought his first vehicle. He coped the New York style of hooking up Jeep Cherokees. The joint was dope. It was all white with a burgundy ragtop, and gold rims. He also had the KC lights with burgundy light covers. Fame was pushing that Huntersville style. He flossed with an all black 190 Benz. We were the stars of every game we walked into.

When we left the game we set outside in a money making circle with all the other local players. The news was out about us but no one really knew the specifics of our money. They knew we were connected to someone heavy but couldn't pin point it because most of everyone in that area had one supplier who we would meet later in our lives. We were having a ball when Daja walked up. Her girl was driving and she asked me if I wanted to get something to eat with her. I knew that meant was I going to treat her but I was like whatever. Money was nothing anyway so I told the crew I would get up with them later. Fame said he wanted to roll too because he was digging Daja's friend. I gave them a "Noize!" chant, and Fame and I left. We went pass the notorious "Hole" first. It was another spot in Norview were dudes were getting money. We met up with one my boys Lil Lucky to grab some weed.

After leaving "The Hole" we went to the waffle house, and pulled in like celebrities. I saw Sammy's jeep and was glad they were there also. Fame, Daja, her friend and I got a table in the corner across from the rest of the crew. We were ordering food for everyone. Fame and I were getting a long great. He wasn't so bad after all.

"Bake, I'm glad you and I got pass all of the beef. You a real cool dude for a Park Place NGHA." I laughed and returned the gesture.

"Yeah, Y'all Huntersville NGHAS ain't that bad." We had a ball that night. Fame took me home and we set up a double date at Flippers the next day.

Instead of going to Auntie's house I decided to go to Grandma Rosa's. Daja and I talked on the phone until 3am. We made it official before we got off the phone. We were now exclusive to each other. I knew in my gut I was making a mistake but my emotions had me locked up like a drug dealer on the 5th floor at 811 East City Hall Avenue (Norfolk City Jail.)

I woke with Daja on the brain. I couldn't wait until we went out that night. I called Fame and he had the plan of getting two rooms at "Motel Six" on Military Highway in Norfolk.

I was with it. All Daja needed to do was come up with a plan to stay out all night.

I called her around 8am. I told her about what Fame and I had planned and she was down. She called her girl on three way and they came up with a lie to tell their parents. I was good because all I had to tell Grandma I was staying over Sammy's.

While I was on the phone Sammy beeped in. I told them I would call them back and we chatted. He was concerned about Daja and I. He knew how news of her cheating effected me and he didn't want anything to effect business. I assured him I wasn't hooked but that was far from the truth. I was enticed again by Daja and he knew it.

The night had come and Fame scooped the girls and me up. He had a bottle of Moet and some strawberries. My man Fame knew what to do when it came to setting up a moment. I have to admit I was still a little green in that department but I was learning. We all shared a room. It didn't matter to the girls. They got in the room, went to the bathroom and came out in sexy lingerie. Fame looked at them and asked if this was their first time and they both laughed. It was apparent it wasn't. I brushed it off because I wasn't going to let my emotions get to me.

We played some Jodeci, and Mary J, and got the night started. That was the night I think started the whole Fame and Daja affair.

When Daja came out of the bathroom I saw how he looked at her and not the shorty he was with. I paid it no mind at first but as the night progressed she and he stared at each other more and more. I wasn't going to let that put a damper on the night so I just brushed it off but it stayed in my mind for a while.

The night progressed and we were all getting bent off Bottles of Moet and weed. We were lit up. Daja asked me to get under the cover with her. When I got under the covers she was buck bald naked. I was rubbing on her bubble like it was crystal ball. It's funny how I didn't see the future. (No pun intended.) She took my clothes off and rubbed my thigh and felt monster. She looked up like she was surprised or either scared one. We did the dam thing and it was hard keeping her quite. As I was hitting her Fame was hitting the other chick. I looked up and this NGHA was looking at me smiling. He was making these wild faces and it took everything in me to keep from laughing. After I got that wiggle in my leg I got up and went to the bathroom. I washed myself off and just stared in the mirror. Daja's joint was bomb! If I wasn't gone before I was then.

We all got up that morning and got breakfast before we departed each other. They were down for doing it again the next weekend. I was down but I told Fame this time we were getting separate rooms because he wasn't going to mess me up with those faces he was making. We all laughed but I wasn't saying that because of the faces to be honest.

I got home at grandmas and Sammy was there. He had this look on his face that I never did like because it meant trouble was coming. He said he had got a call from Big Sippi. He was coming home. He beat the charges. Sammy said his voice wasn't pleasant. In our minds Big Sippi knew we were dealing with someone else. Big Sippi was cool with us and we loved him dearly. I was afraid he would come back and try to shut down Cutta's operation and that was a death sentence. Big Sippi had goons but Big Sippi had soldiers who were willing to kill all in their path. Sammy called an emergency meeting with the crew that night. We all came together trying to figure out what to say to him because the streets were no longer his. Cutta already knew about his release, so we definitely wanted Big Sippi to be easy once he arrived. We all put together some money in a duffle bag for him as a gesture of loyalty. He was on a bus back and would be there in the morning. We had a day to get our plan together. There was one thing I was really worried about. Did Big Sippi turn informant? He was caught with a lot of work so how was he home and not Do-Wop.

Fame was on the same brain wave. Sammy said we just needed to keep a watchful eye and keep Big Sippi at a distance when he got home. It was more for his safety instead of ours. I knew that wasn't going to be easy.

Big Sippi was a go-getter. He left Mississippi with nothing. He built an empire here off love and loyalty.

How were we going to keep him from what he built? How were we going to keep him from something he figured was rightfully his?

After the meeting I talked with Fame for hours about Big Sippi. Do-Wop was his 1st cousin so I knew he felt a different way than all of us about the release of Big Sippi. Fames other cousin "Immortal" was now back out of prison also and that represented another problem. He was a well-known hit-man for the "Village Boys" back in the day. They ran most of the heroin in Norfolk in the very early 80's. He got his name from all of the battles he encountered. He was shot five different times and was of course still living. He worked for an old head name "Big Money" and he murdered him later in the game to take over Norfolk. He was a messy killer. That was his down fall. It took the Police department about a day to figure out it was Immortal. He killed Big Money. His time was cut short when he beat his appeal. How? I have no idea! Fame knew he was going to pose a problem also. The streets were hot enough without all of the drama that was about to hit us.

Fame knew his cousin wouldn't let up once his engine started. He said we were going to have to kill him if we wanted to keep the streets quite. The way Immortal operated he would have the cops flooding because he was messy. I looked at him sideways at first. This was his flesh and blood. How could he murder someone in his own bloodline that easily? Fame then made it all clear to me. He told me Immortal didn't just kill Big money.

"He also killed my Grandfather." He said. Fame's grandfather was a big time minister in Norfolk and the people loved him. The family said he was murdered late one night when he was leaving his church. They said Immortal owed Big Money a large amount of cash for a deal gone wrong and he wanted his money that night. Immortal ran up in the church killed Fame's Grandfather and stole all of the offering money from that Sunday. The cops had a lead and it pointed to Immortal but his alibi was backed up. The family knew it was Immortal but couldn't prove it either and Immortal became an outcast. I understood his viewpoint. If Immortal was still greasy like corner store chicken the problem was bigger than what I expected.

Fame came up with a plot to kill him and I was thinking of a way to keep Big Sippi paid and safe. He wasn't going to be able to run the streets but I thought if I kept his pockets right his urges would be minimized. I spoke with Cutta about the situation briefly and just as I thought. He wanted Big Sippi dead! He didn't even want to deal with the problem. He told me he dealt with Do-Wop but Big Sippi was in PC, so he wasn't able to get to him. The puzzle was finished! I knew it was too good to be true. Cutta had it all planned out from the jump. He knew about us running Park Place and heard about the money flowing through it and wanted it for himself. We were the perfect cover for his operation and that's why we were selected for his team. It just so happen destiny helped him out when we visited New York. The world is truly small.

I never let Cutta know I was amazed. I let him feel like I had a business is business attitude, but what he did was scandalous. If Fame found out it was Cutta who set his people up, he was going to be on the first train smoking to NY. I always knew he couldn't be trusted. Now everything that happened to Fire and Sammy was coming together. Somewhere in there was a set up and it had Cutta's blood all over it.

The conversation I had with Cutta was self-explanatory. Big Sippi was to be exterminated. What were we going to do? Big Sippi wasn't a punk so he just wasn't going to lie down. Cutta called back and told me something I didn't want to hear. He said he had a package for me and to follow the directions to the letter when it arrived. My heart dropped. It was death package and the deliveryman was me? Cutta often use these packages to stage hits but I had only heard about them. I knew how he thought. He picked me because I was the closes thing to Big Sippi. He trusted me. It was the easiest way to murder someone without alarms going off in their head. I wasn't going to do it but I was stuck in an interesting position. Now I had to come up with a plan to get Big Sippi out of there or death was evident.

The package came the next day with directions and 20,000 dollars cash. It was a hired hit and I was definitely the assassin he chose for the job. Big Sippi's death wasn't going to be on my conscious. He wanted Aunt Marisa to pick him up from the Greyhound station downtown Norfolk at 12 pm. It was only two hours left for me to get a plan together or Country was going to have to go. I never told Sammy or the rest of the crew what was going on because I knew Cutta was testing me. I needed to keep his loyalty in my front pocket. He had to know I would roll out for him at the drop of a dime. This was one of the hardest decisions I had ever made. It was a choice that could have left all of the crew dead or I a traitor. The crew meant more to me than Big Sippi so if he didn't listen it was going to be what it had to be.

We all waited at Aunt Marisa's old apartment because we didn't want him to know just yet of our activity. We were sitting on the front steps when he pulled up. He didn't look himself. We thought he was going to be all smiles but that was far from the truth. He was caring a bible and had a jail made cross around his neck. He got out the car and greeting us with the words peace. We were looking at him like he was crazy because Big Sippi had always been a loud and obnoxious guy. We all ran up to him and gave him hugs. We really missed him and we were glad he was home. He finally smiled and said a lot has changed and he really wanted to talk to us about it. Aunt Marisa had some food laid out a long with some Hennessey. He told us it was a blessing to see us and he had been praying for us. What the hell was he talking about? It seems like everybody that gets locked up converts over to Christ or becomes God Body. It was a good start because if he was truly on his Christ swagger I knew he was going to be out of the game.

We all talked about what happen and how he beat his charges. Big Sippi saw a lot from what he told us and after almost being killed inside he heard God s voice tell him he saved him for a reason. He said the reason was to come back and tell us of what could happen if we didn't change our ways. We didn't want to hear it. He had got us into this lifestyle and now that he did a little time he wanted to come home St. Peter. We weren't trying to hear it.

He told us he was going to become a drug counselor and do a "no drugs" tour around Norfolk's heaviest drug infested neighborhoods. We couldn't have that. He said he felt in his heart he wouldn't live but he had to stick to his mission. The party had turned dismal. Big Sippi had plans to go back to Mississippi after he completed his goals. He told us it was time for us to stop. He knew about our New York connect but he didn't know who it was. We were shocked. While we were moving work he was in jail, so how did he know?

The night was coming to an end and Big Sippi was ready to go. He said he had a lot he needed to do so he wanted to go home. Fame and I volunteered to take him. He said his goodbyes and we were out. Fame had just bought a Cutlass Regal he was about to fix up. Big Sippi was joking that he was finally wearing off on us. Fame made a pit stop by City Park. Big Sippi's entire expression changed. He knew what was up. We couldn't let him do what he was about to do. Fame looked at me, and Big Sippi looked at Fame. He didn't even turn around to look at me or even say anything about sitting behind him. He knew you never let anyone sit behind you in a car. "So, this is how it is hey Bake?

"Yeah, sorry it had to be like this but we on a major level now and we can't have you jeopardizing our operation. You should have left us in the crib hustling video games Sippi."

As I looked at the back of his head while listening to his voice tears started to fall from my eyes. I didn't want to do it but I had too. I allowed him to say the Lord's Prayer and by the time he got to Amen it was over. I put two hydro shocks in the back of his skull. We set the car on fire and I called Cutta and told him it was done. He didn't reply to what I had told him he just hung up the phone. I went home with Big Sippi's face on my mind. It was hard to sleep for about a year but as my heart grew colder sleepless night became a thing of the past.

I knew eventually we were going to have to deal with some of Big Sippi's homeboys so we went and nipped that in at the bud quick. Fame and I got them all one by one. We had to tie up all loose ends so nothing would link back to the crew. I know what you're thinking. I have no heart right? I did have a heart once. I think I left it somewhere between losing my mom and saying yes when the mean streets of Park Place ask for my hand in matrimony. Either way it goes I can't get that back. There aren't enough prayers in the world that would undo what I have done. When you grow up you have aspirations of being a police officer, a doctor or a lawyer. On those blocks life didn't give you that choice. I picked up the list of career selections at school and I swear it said, "Are you really kidding me!" Let me translate that for you. It didn't matter what you did in school with your grades. If you were from my hood, death or dealing was the only option! Life showed me that real quick when I opted to try a life without all the deaths and mayhem.

Destiny showed me a little love in the form of drug raids that were shutting down everything in the area. We were out of product but still set on a large amount of money so we didn't sweat it. I hadn't heard from Cutta since we murdered Big Sippi and I really didn't want to talk with him any way. It seemed like we were all going back to being regular teenagers. It seemed.

The summer had come around for us again and I was getting older and wiser by the streets standards. I was still a certified killer, but I wanted desperately to change that attached stigma. My grandmother had a friend who was a professor at Old Dominion University. She told my Abuela about this program called Upward Bound. It was a program that helped students get ready for the transition into college life. I was ready to leave the money and guns behind so I told Sammy I was going to take a break to go to the program. It was cool anyway because we didn't have any work.

"So you're going to be a school boy now huh Baker? You were always the ambitious one out of the bunch."

"You should come too Sammy. You're going to be a senior this year. Don't you want to go to college?"

Sammy just looked at me and smiled. "I do go to college Grimy! We've being going since we were little. It's called the Park Place school of hard knocks, and I'm close to getting my PHD."

That was the way Park Place made you feel. It made you feel hopeless. In Sammy's eyes this was the only way. He didn't see college as an outlet just a letdown.

I got to the program with little expectations. We all stayed in the dorms at Gresham Hall. It was cool. I got to meet some new people and act normal for a change. No one knew me because most all that attended had come from so upscale private schools. I could be a regular guy with them. I left the jewels and fancy gear at home and packed a few Polo's and a couple pair of sneakers. I wanted to be modest and see how a life of regularity felt.

My roommate was a proficient egghead. He went to Cape Henry Collegiate. It was a private school in Virginia Beach and to go there meant your Parents had money. His style was similar to mine. He rocked Polo's I had never seen. It was nothing to him just clothes. We got a long from the jump. His name was Leo Bragga. I knew one day he would be famous with a name like that because what black parent would name her child that. Leo was short for Leonardo. His mom was some big time visual artist who was at the top of the board for the Chrysler Museum.

Leo was a numbers fanatic. His math skills were off the chain. He was also the young Bill Gates of computers and had chosen to attend ODU when he graduated for Computer Science.

"Where are you from Baker? Are you from Ghent or Larchmont maybe?" He was far removed. I was playing the part well, but I wasn't ashamed of where I was from.

"I'm from Park Place. Well my grandmother lives in Colonial place but if you grew up there you hung mostly in Park Place so that's what one would represent."

He was shocked. He didn't see Park Place in my swagger.

"I would have never guessed that. I'm not insinuating you are a thug or anything. Let's just say if Park Place were a movie, you wouldn't fit the roll."

I was glad to hear that for a change. Everywhere I normally went people knew us and feared us. There I fit in. I was just another normal kid looking a better life.

Leo and I unpacked our clothes and we ventured into the front lobby. We met a lot cool people and the girls were high school teacher fly. I can't say they were around the way girls but they looked good despite it. It was one girl in particular that caught my eye and her name was Sarah Thompson.

Sarah was from Connecticut and had moved to Virginia when she was in the 5th grade. She was thick in the hips and had a smile that would melt anger right off your face. She and I were two of the few that went to public school. She was from Norview, and the mean streets of Wellington Oaks. I knew she looked kind of familiar but nothing really struck my memory banks to say I knew her. Sarah was an honor society member. She had a 4.0 G.P.A. and that was better than good for someone from the rough as we say in Va. She looked good but I was really trying to stay on the humble. Daja and I had made a vow to be exclusive and I had full intentions to keep that vow.

Old Dominion was a nice campus. I began to dream of going there. I didn't have any idea of what I would major in but I loved to write so I thought to myself Journalism would make a good start. We all gathered at the Webb Center and were formally introduced into the program by its Director Dr. Fatima Shakur. Dr. Shakur was a fly Black Panther Party looking sister. She had the most beautiful set of locs and a pair of eyes that would mesmerize you like Medusa minus the stone. Dr. Shakur made it clear from the start. The program was not Romper Room, and if any one signed up thinking they were on a summer vacation they needed to leave at once. Structure was what I needed in my life so I wasn't about to leave no matter what the program had in store for me. She was hardcore. No smiles and all business. Majority of us in attendance were of African or Hispanic descent so I guess that's what made her push extra hard on us.

I sat by Sarah and her girls at the orientation. As Dr. Shakur was speaking you could hear their giggles move almost undetected through the air. I was shook because if Dr. Shakur heard them I didn't want her to think it was I, so I tried to get up quietly without making a scene. Dr. Shakur looked at me and said, "Ok brave soul since you have seen fit to interrupt my presentation with your unwillingness to keep still, why don't you come to the front and tell us your name and a little about yourself and life aspirations."

I was embarrassed. What was I going to say up there? Hello, I'm Baker Grimes from park place and my dream was to be the biggest dealer these parts have ever seen? I kept my composure and walked up gracefully.

"Peace to everyone. My name is Baker Grimes and I'm from a neighborhood not far from here. Until this year I never had any dreams of college and until today I really didn't know what I wanted to be in life. My mom is incarcerated for drugs and my father died when I was young. I live with my grandmother who thought it would be a good idea I attended this program. I hope to gain some insight on life and take it back to my peers. Where I'm from we need it because dreams are hard to achieve. Journalism is what I think I would like to do because I love writing. Maybe I can change the circumstances of my area with a pen? Our story needs to be told because sometimes I don't think the world think we really exists."

Everyone was silent. I didn't intend to air all of that out, but it felt good. Dr. Shakur began to clap and so did the rest of her staff. Her serious straight face smiled big and her cheeks added extra effect with a dropping tear. She walked to the podium and hugged me real big and said in my ear,

"Life will become what you design it to be, always remember that!"

Dr. Shakur was all right. The once hard and up tight exterior was now ripped away and she showed me a side I would later come to need.

The orientation was coming to an end and all let loose their dreams and goals. We left and walked back to the dorms. Leo and I talked about life on the way and were interrupted by the same giggles that made me move during the assembly.

"I guess you thought I was going to get you in trouble?" I turned around and it was Sarah.

"No, I just know how destiny works sometimes and I made an executive decision."

She smiled and Leo and I continued walking and talking.

Once back at the dorms, I sat in the front lobby instead of going to my room. Before I Left Dr. Shakur gave me a book named, "Know they self "by Dr. Na'im Akbar. I sat there reading and was engulfed by Dr. Akbar's assessment of education and knowing the capabilities of our own minds. Only if I could apply what it taught and not stayed trained by the streets that wanted to keep me dependent on it for survival.

As I was reading Sarah interrupted me.

"I apologize if you feel I got you in trouble."

"No trouble, I told you I made my own choice and that was the consequence I had to deal with."

I was all too familiar with consequences so it really wasn't a big deal aside from being put on the spot.

"Is there something you want?" I said with a bit of an attitude because she was starting to agitate me.

"No I don't want anything just trying make small talk. Enjoy your book." She walked away and I felt like a dummy. She was just trying to get my attention the entire time. I could have handled it better so I jumped up, ran after her and apologized.

"I'm sorry. I don't talk much to people I don't know and when someone talks to me more than I think the conversation needs I get defensive."

She looked at me and asked, "Is Park Place that Bad?" Her remarks got my attention.

"Do you know me?"

"Of course Baker, who doesn't know you and your crew?"

My sight of staying under the radar was losing its stealth.

"How do you know me?"

"You took my number at a game once, makes me feel good you don't remember."

The world was smaller than I perceived. It all came to remembrance. She was the girl I was talking to when Daja walked up and interrupted me. Wow! How could I forget a face? I prided myself on remembering key things like that because of the business I was in. One false slip and it could be detrimental to one's life.

"I remember! I was talking to you at the Lake Taylor versus Maury game right?"

"I guess you do remember."

We talked until it was time for lights out. The conversation we had was way more intellectual than the one we had at the game. You could say I was in street mode then. She didn't know about my dealings around town. She just knew I stayed fly and had a reputation for being no nonsense.

"It's good to see you smiling Baker; you think we can continue this conversation tomorrow?"
I was with it for sure. We exchanged numbers again and I headed to my room forgetting all about Daja.

The next morning Leo and I got up and prepared for class. It was set up just like a college schedule. I had two in the morning and one in the evening. Dr. Shakur came and checked on me frequently. She said she was moved by my introduction, and wanted to make sure I was using every resource they offered to accomplish my dreams.

"This place is here for you Baker. Anything you need I want you to come to me personally if you have to and we will see it through."
Dr. Shakur reminded me of Queen. I could see her being something like Doctor Shakur when she became older. I loved Dr. Shakur. She was genuinely interested in my success and it was evident. I took the program very serious and aced all of my courses.

It had come time for graduation. Sarah and I kicked it every day and became very close. It seemed out of all the females I dealt with as a youngster, she understood me the most. I was definitely going to keep in touch with her. She was one of those ones my grandmother would call a keeper.

Sammy and the Noize Makers came to my graduation with Abuela. They were drug dealer fly and the spot light was on them and their jewels. Cutta's two goons even showed love and bought me a laptop and a writing journal. I thought that was considerate being our only function together was business.

The walk across stage was over I had the loudest screams out of everyone. Dr. Shakur had this look on her face but it wasn't pleasant. I think she figured it out by looking at the Noize Makers and our two liaisons. After the ceremony was over she walked up to me while I was talking Sarah and the crew. Right as she walked up Sammy handed me a G stack, and told me it was for all my hard work. "I see hard work pays off hey Baker?" Dr. Shakur said with a smirk. "Introduce me to your comrades." Sammy introduced himself before I could say anything and so did the rest of the crew while Cutta's boys drifted off into the distance.

"I love the garments; I bet they cost a pretty penny." We all knew what she was getting at. Once you looked at us it really wasn't hard to tell. Drug dealers had this fresh money look you could often pick from a mile away.

"Yeah we stay fly, my Grandmother spoiled Grimy and me...I meant Baker and I."

She knew what was up. Dr. Shakur wasn't a fool. She grew up in Marcy Projects in New York. After high school she attended Columbia University and later went on to Stanford for grad school. She knew the look and smell of dope money. I remember her having conversation with me about her brother who was murdered in the Bronx because of a drug deal gone bad. She vowed then to never see another love one under her care die to drugs again.

"I'll be keeping in touch with you Baker. Design your life to your dreams specifications. I'm very proud of you."

Dr. Shakur hugged me like she was afraid she would never see me again. I knew that kind of hug well.

I was more than convinced the game was over for me. I didn't want any part in it any more. I wanted to achieve what I knew I could do. I wanted a PHD just like Dr. Shakur and teach creative writing in my spare time to kids in low-income neighborhoods. Writing was the perfect psychiatrist.

It came time for me to pack my bags. Sammy and the crew were on their way back to Park Place. Leo and I had a chance to chat a while and laugh at all the good times we had while in the program.

"You a real cool dude Leo!"

"You too Baker, call me any time good friend. We should stay in touch."

I concurred. Leo was the type of change I needed. I wasn't going to dump the crew but all of our activities; I wanted no more parts in.

Baker Grimes
Hamza Atoi
CHAPTER EIGHT

The program was a beautiful change of scenery, but I was more than glad to be back amongst the crew minus the hustle. Park Place in that minimal time had once again changed. The streets seem vacant. The normal traffic that once moved constantly throughout the blocks was almost non-existent, and those familiar faces that walked the streets day and night were gone. "Let me tell you what's been happening since you've been gone."

He began to tell me about the continuing drug raids that had been taking place.

"The cops have been hitting spots from 35th and Newport to 27th and Gosnold."

"Nobody got any work besides us, but they don't know it."

Sammy continued to give me the run down about the operation the cops were using to clean up the streets. He also said that Cutta was about to send some of his boys. He was sending them so we could capitalize further off the sweeps the narcotics police were making.

"We're not affected by it at all Bake, we gone be alright! If anything, we are going to eat more,"

Sammy said with exuberance in his voice. He was sitting with three bricks in a bag under his bed, and that explained why. He showed it to me when I first got home, and then gave me the run down I just told you.

We had survived the drug raid because we were only pushing heavy weight to two people. I told Sammy about the changes that I was trying to make in my life.

"I know you want to stop Bake, but I need you more than ever now!"

I had never told Sammy no before. If he needed me then I knew he really meant it because he never asked a lot of me. The problem was, neither of us had a need for this life, but I guess we were too deep to swim our way out.

"Anything for you Sammy."

The nail was in the coffin. It was no hope of us getting out now. The forces of evil were definitely battling over who would have ownership of my life. Everything was moving like we wanted it to. What happened next I never expected.

The Noize Makers and I were at our high schools basketball game versus Booker T. Washington. The game was at their gym and that was Fame's stomping ground. We all walked in with our jewels shining and then the unimaginable happened. Cutta walked in with a crucial goon squad, but right behind him was Hush. Hush looked up and immediately looked towards where I was sitting. He smiled, tapped Cutta on the shoulder, and then pointed to us. It didn't look right. Hush and Cutta together made no sense. In my mind it was definitely time to stay on point because something was surely about to jump off.

Cutta and hush walked to our section with their gorillas, and sat down. "What's up Sammy? What's up Grimy? You all are looking real fresh."

I returned the greeting to Cutta, but Sammy just stared like he saw a monster.

"What gwan Sammy? You don't have any love for me?" Sammy immediately snapped out of it.

"I'm just zoning, you know I got love for you Cutta."

He reached over and gave him dap. Sammy seemed on edge. He was now on guard. What was he thinking? I wished I could pick his thought.

"Aye Bake, you want anything from the concession stand?"

"No I'm good." Sammy then looked at Hawk and gave him the eye.

Hawk got up,

"I want something."

They both got up. Then Clarkboy followed. "What's been up Grimy, I got some big things in the works for your crew and you."

"Like what?"

"It's big, you all are about to be put on bigger than Big Sippi ever envisioned. Hush is down with us now too." Hush looked over at me like he wanted to say something, but Cutta began talking about his plans again.

"All dem other hustler dem done. I and I bout to put breaks pon dem pussyclatt."

"Wait and see Grimy we bout to be gods!"

Half time had come and Sammy was still at the concession stand with Clarkboy and Hawk.

"What's taking them NGHA's so long? They're missing Booker T. shoot the lights out on us," Tony said with excitement. I looked around to see if I saw them.

"Let's go and see what's up Tony," I said with concern. We both got up and proceeded to the hallway where the concession stand was located. Sammy was out pacing the floor like he was ready to kill someone.

"What's up Sammy?"

He didn't answer me he just continued talking to himself under his breath like I wasn't there. Hawk said that he had been like that the entire time they been in the hall.

"Whatever is up Sammy, you need to dead it until later!" He looked at me, and stared deep into my eyes as if to say later it will definitely be dead. I then knew that someone out of Cutta's goon squad had something to do with what happen to Sammy in New York, and if that was indeed true, they were going to be dead before they got home.

Half time had come and gone. We all went back inside and sat back down. Sammy took my advice, and put on airs. You could tell that he was ready for war.

"Aye Cutta, what y'all got going on after this?"

'It's whatever, what you youths trying to do.

"Are you all hungry?"

We all nodded in unison. Sammy looked at me and grinned. He had some sort of plan in his head and it was going to be executed with haste.

"As a matter of fact, we got some shit we need to take care of after the game, so we'll get back at you later tonight."

The one good thing about our crew was we knew each other's moves, so no one questioned each other's decisions. We all were ride or die.

"That's cool, make that money youth, and call me later." We all got up and left before the game was over. On our way out we ran into Fame.

"What up Bake?"

"I'm cooling Fame, what up with you?"

"Nothing at all. Who were them NGHA y'all were politicking with? Those NGHAS look like killers."

"They just some people we know from New York."

"So what you about to get into Fame?

"We about to take care of some shit, are you down?"

"You know me I'm always with it!"

Fame looked at his boys and told them that he would get up with them later.

"So what's the deal Bake, what y'all got going on?"

"Remember the SHT that happen to Sammy in New York? Sammy thinks one of the NGHAS with the dude we know did it." Sammy then blurted out that he didn't think anything. He knew that was the NGHA, but he wasn't ready to do anything yet.

"We have to sit on this for a minute because it has to be done right!"

"Which one was it," hawk asked?

Sammy didn't say anything. I then asked,

Which one Sammy?" He looked and said with a low tone,

"You all will know when the time is right!"

My mind was racing. I didn't know who it could have been. I knew it couldn't have been Hush, or Cutta, but I was taught not to put anything pass any one. He said in the hospital it was all a blur so how could he pick anyone out of the bunch? I knew he wouldn't lie but it was hard to figure out who it could have been since the other dudes he saw where history. In the game there is no loyalty. Whoever did it was a dead man that was for sure.

I got a page from Cutta later that night.

"Aye Sammy it's Cutta, we need to get to a phone booth and see what he wants."

We all walked to the phone booth at that Burger King across the street from Curry Park.

"What up yout? I need you to do me a favor, and it's BIG! Gather all your other youth dem and meet at the *Town Point Hotel* on VA. Beach blvd.

"We right over here now. We're at the Burger king across the street."

"Stay there my youth, we link up."

I wondered what was going on.

'Is everybody strapped?"

I asked the crew. Everyone nodded.

"Cutta on his way here, he said to post up until he gets here."

The wait was short, but the anxiety made it seem as if years were passing.

What's taking them so long?"

It's only been five minutes Bake, calm down kid,"

Sammy said patiently. Cutta and his crew pulled up caravan style, one Benz behind another.

"What up Grimy, get in let's take a ride. You get in with me and Hush Baker, you too Sammy."
Sammy and I got in, and the rest of the crew got in with his boys in the other two cars.
"Where we going Cut?" I asked.
"We bout to link up with these moneymakers out Va. Beach."
Who are they?"
You ask to many questions my lad. What happen to our trust?"
Hushed looked at me and just nodded. He never said too much of anything verbally, but his actions always spoke loud. He was saying be easy.

We pulled up to a hood called *Bayside Arms*, and Arms was right. This was one of the few hoods in Va. Beach that really was ready for war. I remember Fame telling us about his boy that ran Bayside Arms. It was some Panamanian NGHA rightfully named Panama Gonzales. Rumor went he was sitting on boulders. Cutta wasn't a fool. He knew if someone was getting money like him, he wanted to be a part of it.

Virginia Beach was a different type of hustle because they had a different type of clientele. They had that white money. Most of their heavy customers were doctors, lawyers, dentist, and even V.B.P.D. Can you believe that? These NGHA actually had cops with the sniffles. They also had delegates and judges on their pay roll. Imagine those ordinary street hustlers with that much power. Cutta definitely had a plan.

Once we stopped, Cutta's goon squad got out first. They looked around and headed towards these dudes that were on the block. They spoke briefly then one of Cutta's boys looked at the jeep we were in and nodded.

"Let's go youth, Cutta said.

"Let's go and expand our empire."

We all got out and followed the NGHA Cutta's goon was talking to. We got to the apartment, and this big grizzly dude answered the door before we could knock on it.

"He in the back waiting."

Grizzly Adams took us to the back where this little NGHA was sitting with three chicks around him like he was Tony Montana.

"What up Cutta? I heard a lot about you, have a seat." Panama didn't look like the tales spoke of. I thought I was going to see this 40-year-old dude with scars on his face, and a cigar hanging from his lip. No, that wasn't him at all. This wasn't a movie. This was real.

Panama looked like your average Joe, but with a dope sense of fashion. He had two gold teeth in his mouth that shined like the sun. He had one on each side, next to his front teeth.

"So how you wanna share this? This game is you scratch my back and I'll scratch yours. You inching?" Panama said with a grin.

"I'm definitely itching B, the question remains rude boy, are you ready to scratch?"

"Say no more friend it's done."

Just like that the deal was closed. How it would work, I don't know, and I guess it wasn't meant for me to know. Sammy and I were puzzled. As we walked back to the jeep, Sammy looked at Cutta and asked

"What just happen?"

"We just made a deal that your kids and their kids are going to be able to eat off for years."

The scene was getting to deep. We were too young to be in the game like that. How in the hell do young NGHA's like us hide all that money we were making? My grandmother already knew something was going on, but this was really going to verify it. I admit the lifestyle was what I wanted. I love being able to buy what I wanted to buy at anytime, but was it worth it? I mean you had to watch out for the Feds, stick up boys and those scheming broads whose goal was to try and get your dough by any means. FCK it was what I wanted to say. I snapped my thoughts out of that way of thinking quickly. I wasn't going to be one of those paranoid old heads with a bundle of money, but too messed up in the head to spend it. I wasn't hustling for that. It was the freedom that I love. It was the free will!

Cutta told us that he was going to leave Hush with us, so he could oversee everything. You know, make sure it ran proper. I was definitely cool with that. I knew Hush would look out for us. He was cool. Cutta also left two new goons. He told us when everything came together he was going to give us a call. I was ready for whatever. First thing was first; we had to get off what we were sitting on.

The next day Cutta caught a flight back to New York to set things up for the new connect, and then it clicked. Why the FCK are we getting a new connect? The one we had I know was more connected than this young Panamanian NGHA. I bust my brain thinking about it all because if something had gone wrong, we would inherit that beef too. Maybe that's why he employed Hush. Hush was true killer. If something ever popped off he was the one you wanted in your crew. He was the black terminator, but Hush and Cutta once had beef, so you can imagine how baffled I was.

Don't get me wrong. This new connect was plugged in, but the one we had was the ultimate in my eyes. I guess it was going to be what it was! All I was concerned about was the money.

A couple weeks had passed since we last saw Panama. We also hadn't heard from Cutta, so we just continued to do what we do. We got rid of the three bricks we had, so all we could do now was wait for Cutta to give us the word.

Since everything was at a standstill.

We decided it was time for the crew to go out and hit the block. I called Grandma Rosa and I told her that Sammy and I were going to the movies, and we were going to stay at Aunt Marisa. She told me to be safe and keep my eyes out for signs. I should've known right there. That was a sign to stay in the house.

It was a Friday night and the jump off spot was mid-city bingo hall. Soul Ranger hosted it. He was a local DJ for the radio station W.R.A.P. I called up the crew and everyone was at my Aunt's Crib within the hour, and ready to go. We called a cab and we were out. When we got there it was jumping. Chicks were everywhere, and we were looking fresh. The Dookie chains we had on made NGHA's jealous as hell, but we didn't care! Me especially. I was waiting for one of them to try me. Grand always told me be careful for what you ask for!

We were all standing on the wall macking to some chicks we had just met, and up walks Lee-Lee. Yeah, I'm talking about the NGHA that I was about to thrash at Flippers.

"What up Bake?"

"What up Lee?"

He was looking at me like he wanted to do something.

"What's on your mind Lee-Lee, you good?"

"I'm always good! How Your BTCH doing?"

"What? What the FCK you just say NGHA"

"You know that fine BTCH you had with you at Flippers?"

Right then, without hesitation, I smacked the SHT out of him. We start stomping him like we were trying to put out a fire. The security team ran up and saw that it was us, and instead of breaking it up, they helped out. Each stomp flashed the future in my face. I knew I had messed up, but that's how I got down. No one was going to disrespect me. The stomp out only lasted about a minute, but it felt like it was never going to end. When everyone scattered, Lee-Lee, and two of his boys were laid out on the floor. We all ran outside and amazingly enough we saw Hush in a van. He waved his hand over for us to get in and we were out.

"Grimy you smarter than that. All that madness ain't good for business," Hush said calmly.

Everyone was silent. On the real, I think we all knew Hush was right 'because no one said anything all the way home. I guess we all had time to reflect on what we did. I myself knew that a windstorm was going to come from it, but it was too late to worry about it.

Baker Grimes
Hamza Atoi
CHAPTER NINE

Weeks went by and still no call came from Cutta. We had no product and the crew was starting to get restless. Sammy was walking around the house most of the time talking to himself. He looked like he was losing it. Honestly, he had never been the same since New York. I would observe him looking out the window laughing, aiming his gun like he was a sniper. He would mumble, and rock while watching television, and was heavily into old time murder movies. All I could do was make sure that he wouldn't go off the deep end. Whatever was happening to him, I knew he needed some kind of help before it was too late. As for me, I was kind of happy that we were out of product. I felt like a regular kid again.

During the break I decided to go and stay with Grand until things popped back off. It also gave me time to ease her worries because I was never home with her. While I was there she acted as if I had never been gone, and not one time did she ask or nag me about my activities while I was away. I think she already knew. What I never understood is why she never said anything to me about it. Maybe she could have saved me, or maybe she knew that I was going to do what I wanted. Don't get me wrong, I wasn't a disrespectful kid; I was just a free spirit, and I think that was where the problem was.

For some reason Daja was heavily on my mind. I hadn't been out with her since I got back from the program. She called me a couple of times, but of course, I was busy. I decided this would be a good time to go out and spoil her with gifts. I called her and her sister answers the phone like she was up to something.

"Hello?"

"What up shorty girl where's your sister?"

"Huh...who?"

"Your sister, who else would I be talking about?"

"Oh...hey Baker... um... she not here.

In the background I could hear her and a male voice laughing. They must have thought I was some kind of dumb NGHA.

"Aight, tell her I called, and I got something for her. No, I'm going to bring it to her. I'm on my way!"

I knew that would get the truth out of her.

"Hold up Bake, she walking in the door now."

Daja picked up the phone.

"Hey baby, where have you been?"

I knew right then that she was on something sneaky, so I didn't answer her, I just told her I was on my way, and I had something for her. She called me back, as soon as I hung up. I let it ring and just sat there. My Grand screamed downstairs for me to answer it, but I told her it was a telemarketer. Daja never did know how to lie. I continued to wait. I knew if she came over my house within ten minutes, she was up to no good. The doorbell rung, it happen just like I thought it would. I took my time getting to it. When I got to the door, I just stared at her.

"Hey boo, you gone let me in?"

I opened up the door and began to calm myself down, so I could throw her off the trail and catch her later.

"Sister said you had something for me?"

I went in my pocket and pulled out five hundred dollars because I really didn't have anything for her. She then began to tell me I was the greatest boyfriend in the world. I was numb because I knew she was up to something. I just couldn't prove it at the time.

I remember talking to Hawk when I was in New York. He told me Daja was fooling around. I never really forgot it. It always stayed at the back of my mind. I guess that's what really made me mad when Lee-Lee said what he said.

It's funny how dudes get mad at their girls for things they're doing, but if a chick do the same thing we get bent out of shape. I guess that's the way it goes.

I continued to be in a relationship with Daja regardless because I knew I did dirt also, and I wasn't about to let her get me heated.

The night we stomped Lee-lee was on my mind heavy. Normally when that happened it was a warning sign for the future, but I was so caught up in being gully, I didn't pay it any attention.

One night I got a call from Fame, he said that he needed to talk to me about what happened to Lee-Lee. I don't know why I snapped at Fame, but I did. I really didn't want to hear it. He was only trying to tell me to keep my eye open because they were plotting. I kept a tool on me so I was ready for whatever they wanted to do. I don't regret much but not talking to Fame about what happen was a mistake. I knew he could have eased the situation. It's messed up that I had to kill him too. He was close to Lee-Lee plus other factors. Damn! I know it sounds crazy but I really wish he were still here.

Why you looking at me like that? Oh…I thought you knew I killed Fame. Females and money will make you do some wild things. I really felt like I had to do it. Fame was crew, but he grew up with them dudes. Do you really think he was going to choose me over them?

If Sammy were here, he would tell you I did over Daja, but that's far from the truth. Although I did have an instinct that led me to believe they were sexing each other, but I never did find any real proof. Who cares? It is what it is now. Since we're at this point in the story I might as well tell you what happen…

One day all of us got together and went to the movies. This was when the Movie Theater was outside of Military Circle mall. We really weren't trying to see the movie. We where there for show. A lot of things were running through my mind. It was the crew, Fame and I. The whole entire time, I had my eye on Fame. He looked different to me. I don't know if it was because I had an idea that he and Daja were up to no good. I wanted to talk to Fame like a man about the situation, but him being the NGHA he was, I knew he would just laugh me off.

I can't remember what movie we went to see. I guess that's because I wasn't paying it any mind. I do remember Fame sat on the other side of Daja. I was heated. It set me off. I never said anything until later, right before I put two in the back of his head. The whole movie was a blur. My mind was flipping, and all I could see was Daja and Fame on the screen kissing each other. I thought it was the weed, but weed always made me relaxed. I knew right then. I was going to murder him before it was all over, and I did!

You know what? I don't need to rush the story. Let's stay on the path...cool? Alright my friend, remember when we went to see the Panamanian kid? Well, destiny had it all planned out for us. Him and I linked up, not by chance of course, but the way life intended for it to happen. Fame and I was at the Bayside and Maury high basketball game. We normally didn't hang less than five in the crew, but we had such a name that we didn't care anymore. As usual we were looking fresh. Gold around our necks and covering our fingers like we were the descendents of King Midas. As soon as we walked in, we caught the attention of Panama. He was sitting in the stands with two females on the side of him and four goons in front ready to kill something if they had to.

He motioned for us to come to where he was sitting. The crowd moved like Moses parting the Red Sea. Panama had the much respect.

"¿Qué pasa Baker?

"Nada"

" Tú comprendes español?

"¡Yo soy Dominicana! Se puede harblomos ínglés ahora?"

Sammy always said I had a smart mouth and one-day it would get me in trouble.

"So are you all ways this tough?"

"That's what they say!"

Panama just paused and stared at me for a second. The look he gave me was saying that he and his bodyguards were going to beat the hell out of me after the game and place me in a dumpster somewhere in Bayside Arms. I stared right along with him and so did Fame. That's why I liked Fame. He was ride or die no matter the circumstances. After a minute of intense eye contact, Panama began to smile

"That's why these little NGHA's getting money. They don't have fear."

He began to tell us that he needed people like us on his team. I thought it was a set up to see were my loyalty stood, so I told him that we were good with Cutta. His face expression changed and you could tell that it wasn't a trick question.

"I don't mean any disrespect, but I really don't trust your boss."

"What does that mean," I asked with a temper.

He proceeded to tell me about what he heard happen to us in New York. He told me that he always kept his ear low to the ground because that's where the truth could be heard. If he was being honest, it was time for some answers, but if he was deceiving me, I was placing Sammy and I in a world a trouble. I began to ask him questions like I was really concerned about what he knew. I was trying to manipulate the conversation so he would tell me exactly what I needed to hear. He did!

"The word is, Cutta set up you and your cousin up so he could duck out on his connect."

He told me that it was the oldest trick in the book. Oshun and Asia were pawns and didn't even know it. I was heated but I made sure I didn't show any emotion just in case it was a set up by Cutta to see if I was on to him. On the inside I was a ball of rage. I knew he had to know something because only people that were close to me knew of our trip to New York. All I could see was how it all unfolded. I began to think back. Maybe he was being honest. I still couldn't take any chances. I knew how Cutta operated. His intellect surpassed what appeared to others as street knowledge. I had to make sure, so I told him I appreciated his info, but I would need to investigate for myself, and I would get back to him. Then he said something that had me bugging.

"Just let Hush know what you want to do and we'll make things happen." I was truly puzzled. Hush was supposed to be working for Cutta. It was driving me mad trying to figure it out.

When I got home, I went straight to my room sprawled on my bed to think. Everything Panama told me made sense, but why let Sammy live, and not his brother? I guess it would make the plot more believable. If he could do that to his own brother, I knew my life meant nothing to him. Cutta was way more advanced and had a lot more manpower. I couldn't just hit him up any type of way. If I were going to kill him it was going to take a master plan. Of course, with my sick mind it didn't take long to figure one out.

The drug game was getting more difficult. I had a lot of decisions to make, and I couldn't let anyone know about my moves, so I could assure that my plans would not be interrupted. It was time to call Cutta and see what was going on. We hadn't heard from him since the meeting.

I called him for a week straight but I got no answer. No one had seen or talk to him. I spoke with Hush and Hush told me that's how he operated. Sometimes he would disappear and lay low. During that time, I kept in constant contact with Panama. To keep him close I would do disposal work for him. I never pushed any dope for him because I was still trying to appear loyal. I became his number one hit man, and my lust for blood was growing. Panama took care of me, and in return I kept him safe. I even knocked off his number one goon. I did it without his permission, but I had to. It was the only way to get right by his side.

After a while, he began to let me in on all of his deals. The pieces that I needed for my puzzle were coming together. I found out who Panama's connect was and the connect Cutta schemed. I moved in silence every time I was in New York. Cutta had eyes everywhere, so I knew I would have to find out soon before my luck was depleted.

One thing I didn't factor in was Cutta and his goons. I knew I was going to have to lay them down also. The only one I had to worry about was Hush. He looked out for me before, but was he on my side or was he loyal to Cutta? I had to think of a way to keep Hush out of the equation, and I had to be smart because Hush could smell bull crap a mile away.

It was time to call the crew and let them know what I had planned. Once I told them, they all looked at me like I was planning to kill Cutta. I guess killing his men was just the same to them. I told them that it was for the good of our situation.

"Look, I don't know what this dude is up to, but I got some info that I know is true."

Sammy looked at me with bright eyes. He had this wicked smirk on his face like he knew what Panama told me was indeed fact and now it was finally payback time.

"Bake is right," Sammy said with a sinister grin, and then went into a corner and sat to himself. If I didn't kill them boys for any other reason it would be for what they did to my primo.

No one went against the grain with what I had to say. They knew if I said it, it needed to be done. It went without questioning. I set up the entire plan, and I told them it had to be done on the next day. I told you fate had all ways been in my favor.

Before we set out to do what we had to do, we got a call from Hush. He told me that he had to go back to New York on some other business and he would be back in three days. I smiled from ear to ear. I was happy because if I had to, I was willing to kill Hush also. I know it would have been bad, but it was whatever it took to get the job done. The next day came and Hush was on a plane back to N.Y.

I called up the Noize Makers and told them it was time. We waited until nightfall, and made a bogus call to Cutta's boys about the strip party that Fame and his people were putting on at Town Point Hotel. Sammy called two chicks that would do anything for him, and it was on. Once Cutta's boys got there, we waited for the signal. We were all in an adjoining room next door. The girls that Sammy got were perfect. Hollywood actresses couldn't have done a better job. Then the signal came.

"Are y'all ready to get this?"

The adjoining door opened, and we ran in with guns drawn. They looked at us puzzled then before they could speak it was over. We just stood back and watched the girls do their thing amazon style. After it was all done. We all left out in ten-minute intervals. Phase one of my plan was over. I could now concentrate on the rest of my plan, now that they were out of the picture.

The next day I got a call from Panama. I knew he was calling me about what happened last night because it was all over the news. He was going off about how things were really going to be hard now. I didn't understand, but later in the conversation it made sense.

The two dudes we murdered were more than just henchmen. They were Federal agents on Cutta's payroll. The heat was really about to come down. We knew that Norfolk and all the surrounding cities were going to be buzzing with federal agents. I was shook. If you know anything about the Feds, you had to know they would stop at nothing to a find out who murdered one of their own. I called up Sammy and told him we needed to find out where the girls who did the work were. Fate like always was on my side, so I had a plan. I wasn't sure it would work, but it was worth a try. One of girls we used for the hit also checked us in the room. Fame had a good hook up with one of the Hindu Indian cats that owned the hotel, so he called in a favor. The cameras they had at the front desk helped our plot even more. Now all we had to do was find the two girls and kill them.

We had to make it all look like a robbery. We picked them up from the Bridle Creek neighborhood in Virginia Beach. Sammy and I made them think we were going to hit them off with some work because they were getting money in the Creek. I even took a deposit on the work they never would see. We laid them down and left evidence that would link them to the murders at Towne Point.

Panama called me about five days later and told me they found the girls who murdered the agents, but we still had to lay low until the Feds cooled down. That was all right with me. It was at the end of the school year anyway and during that time I was on a murdering frenzy so it was good to wash my hands and act civilized for a change. I asked my grandmother if it was ok to go back to New York and chill with Celia and Uncle Flip for the summer. Once I got the go ahead, I packed my bags and set my sights on NY.

Baker Grimes
Hamza Atoi
CHAPTER TEN

This time Sammy decided to stay at home with the crew and wait for the word from Cutta. I knew the trip wasn't going to end up as a vacation. My life wasn't set up that way any longer. Once I got to Uncle Flip's, I saw who I had been looking for the whole time. It was Cutta.

"So where you been Cutta? I asked with sarcasm.

He looked at me like he didn't want to answer. I don't think he knew I was going to be there.

"I have to answer to you now my youth?"

He was up to something because his answer had mad hostility behind it. He began to tell me it was hot and the Feds were up to something, so it was time to lay low.

"Trust me little man, I know what's up and every man gone get what's do when we resume business!" His statement bothered me. He left without even saying goodbye to Celia or me. I knew he was on to us or he had an idea of what was going on. If he did I was in mad danger. I didn't even get a chance to peep his body language. He left so fast! He was as crafty as I was when it came to manipulation. We both knew how to play mind games. We used our gift to make people tell us what we wanted without even knowing what we were doing. I knew Cutta was watching me.

The part that was puzzling was the fact that the Feds were on him. He was normally more careful than that. He had to know they were Feds because I have seen him eyeball them a mile away. Plus he had inside men who he paid very well that worked for the Feds; like the two dudes we murdered. Something definitely wasn't right and I was going to get down to the bottom of it all.

I tried to put Cutta at the back of mind. I didn't want it to consume me. I knew what I had to do, but it was going to be handled in due time.

Two weeks had passed and it seemed as if I was headed toward a normal summer for a teenager. Celia and I were having a ball. Right when normal and I were becoming friends, he left, and my crazy cousins from Miami, Sosa and Solo arrived. They were 18 and 19 years old. Both looked older. If you took a glance at them from a distance, they looked like twins. Both were about six foot four, dark skinned and chiseled like they were He-man action figures. Sosa was the rowdiest one. Everything he said was followed with...MTHRFKR. They grew up in Miami. I use to hear about all of the crazy things they'd do, but I had never talked to them or even seen them in person until then. Celia had also told me that they hated Cutta because they hooked him up with a Dominican connect in Miami and he never hit 'em off for the link. I smiled at that because I knew it would be a plus in what I wanted to do.

Sammy wasn't there but I still had back up. Solo, Sosa and I were getting aquatinted well. I was younger than them both, but it never stopped us from partying together because everyone knew me. I was Celia's cousin and Cutta's little man!

A lot was still in my head from my last trip to N.Y., and Oshun was one of them. I wondered if she was still living in New York. I wondered was she still alive!

One day Sosa and I were sitting on the stoop, watching uncle play chess with his buddies when an angel walked by. It was Queen. She heard that I was back in town and decided to come see me. I hadn't seen her since that last trip. She was still beautiful as ever.

"¿Que pasa papi?

"¿Que pasa preciosa, cómo estes?"

"Good, now that I know you're back. Her words sound like heaven speaking to me. Each sound drew me closer to her lips. Queen was always my top choice when it came to a mate. She was bold yet humble. She was the type of girl that I needed, but I was afraid for her. I knew what I was destined for, and I didn't want her to be a part of it. Queen was already trapped because of her older brother, so I didn't want to add to her problems because I found out early in the game, when someone wants you and they can't reach you they will grab the closes thing to you.

I was glad to see her. I knew it couldn't be the way I wanted it to be, but I could have fun and live for now, so I asked her out.

"Let's get out for old time sake?"

"O.K."

It was always cut and dry with Queen. She was a yes or no type of girl, and she never beat around the bush.

"Can my cousins roll? They're here from Miami and I want to show them a good time." She agreed and we all went to Manhattan to chill.

My cousins were amazed, but they felt right at home because New York was as rowdy as they were. Sosa was hyped up and wild as ever. He wouldn't shut up. I could tell that Queen was becoming annoyed by his behavior, so I did everything that I could to keep her attention off of him. I could feel it in my gut it was turning bad. While I was trying to calm down Sosa and keep Queen cool, Solo was watching me.

"Ain't nothing like family primo."

I looked at him before I answered. I knew he had some kind of underline statement, but of course I was smart, and hip to all types of sarcastic statements.

"Yeah primo, ain't nothing like family." Solo was taking up for his brother. Every time Queen would look at Sosa, Solo would look at her. Then it happened.

"Where that BTCH NGHA Cutta at?" The car grew silent.

Queen's expression grew hostile. She was always a smart and intelligent girl, so she said nothing that would let them know that she was related. Cutta raised both his sister and brother, so they knew what to do and what not to do. I was in a rock and a hard place because my cousins were loud mouths. I just knew Sosa was going to say he wanted to see Cutta for bouncing on them and not paying for the connect. I didn't want Queen to know that I had plans to kill her brother, so I quickly maneuvered into the conversation and changed it up.

"Why the hell you asking about dudes? You need to be asking were the girls at."

It worked. They both began asking Queen if she had any friends that love rowdy boys. It wasn't over by far, and that I could tell by Queen's facial expressions. I needed to think of a way to keep her from telling her brother that my cousins were asking about him and I needed to find a way fast.

The day went by quickly. Queen took us back to the house, but I didn't want to get out of the car until I could feel her intentions.

"Hey primos. Go in the house I'll be up there in a minute."

They both got out, but not before Solo closed the car door he gave Queen a stare like he knew whom she was.

"I think your cousin doesn't like me?"

"No, not true. He's like that with everyone."

I did what I could to take her mind off Solo. All I needed was Cutta finding out they were asking about him. He was always the paranoid type. He wouldn't hesitate killing them for sure.

We sat in the car for about an hour kissing and talking about old times. I didn't want them coming back down stairs looking for me, so I cut it short. By that time I knew I had her mind off of what Solo said.

"Will we see each other tomorrow Mama?"

She nodded and gave me a long kiss good night, but I didn't like it. I could tell that my plan didn't work. She was going to talk to Cutta about it. I just knew it, but I couldn't sweat it.

That whole entire night I was paranoid. I didn't want it to happen like this because if had to kill Cutta while I was in New York everyone would know.

The next morning I called Queen early. I think it was about five in the morning. It was all in attempt to see if she talked to her brother. When you wake a person up before they get all of their rest, their mind tends to be a bit boggled. I let the phone ring until she answered it.

"Hello...who is this, and do you know what time it is?"

"Queen...its Baker. I'm sorry that I'm calling you so early. I just couldn't wait to hear your voice."

"You could have waited until it was later in the morning Baker. I'm tired."

I immediately started running game, telling her a voice like hers didn't have a time limit on it. I needed to know if she talked to her brother and time was of the essence.

"So, did your brother get back yet?"

"No, you know how he is Bake, in and out like a ghost, who knows where he is."

I was safe for that moment. If she had talked to her brother I would have instantly picked up on it. Queen was my girl. I really and truly loved her. In all actuality, she should have been the mother of my son, but you know destiny is a jealous BTCH on her period, so of course it didn't work out that way. One thing was certain, I needed to ease Queen's anger before she talked with her brother or it was going to be a war!

I knew deep in my heart that Sosa and Solo was going to be trouble. They were just too wild, and hot heads like them were bad for family business.

I think that particular trip to New York is what created the monster that sits before you. All of the incidents that took place on that trip placed me in a state of pure, unadulterated hate! I never intended to do any of the things I did, and if it weren't for those two Neanderthals, I never would have!

Well, I know the suspense is killing you and you're wondering what I'm talking about. Let me start by saying this! What I'm about to tell you is off the record.

That night I can't shake. I can see the blood flow and I can hear the screams fresh in my ears. I have asked God to forgive me but I don't think I have yet to forgive myself! Sosa and Solo put me in the worst decision making position of my life. If they were here now I would hesitate to kill them again!

I told you, Solo was as smart as I was. I should have known that he was thinking on my level. Allowing Queen to talk to her brother would have been a major problem, and we both knew it! I don't know where it all went wrong or where I slipped but the next set of events spelled doom for my soul!

I remember the night it happened. The moon was burnt orange, eerily covered by light clouds. The smell of the air was morbid. It was like death was setting the stage for what was about to take place.

Sosa and Solo asked if I wanted to go to this party with them in Washington heights. I decided to stay home and play chess with Celia. I hadn't spent any time with her since I had got back to New York. We ordered pizza, played chess and watched movies until we fell asleep. It started as a normal night, but normal was a stranger I had yet to meet. The phone rang. I rolled over, letting it ring a couple of times thinking Celia would get up to answer it, but when I looked around; I saw that she was in a deep sleep. It was odd. Celia never slept that hard, as a matter of fact I had never slept that hard before either! We played chess until our fingers were tired and drank wine and watched movies until we fell asleep, and then it hit me! The wine! I remember Celia being mad because she said Cinda had opened up her bottle of chardonnay, But we now know it was Solo or Sosa. He put something in the wine before he left because Celia said she was going to drop by the party to check on them. He didn't want that to happen because of what they plotted.

I answered the phone.

"Hello", I said with a half sleep voice.

"Hey primo we need to get out of New York right now!"

I knew instantly they had done something horrible!

"What the hell man, what's going on?"

Solo said with a calm and nonchalant voice,

"Cutta had to get this primo!"

At first I was mad because I wanted the pleasure of killing Cutta myself. Plus, before I had fulfilled my plan to eliminate him, I was going to solidify my ties with his connect so we would be straight financially.

"Where the hell are you two?"

"We're In Brooklyn inside the old warehouse Uncle owns."

Now how in the hell did they know about the warehouse Uncle Flip really didn't own! They were two dummies. The warehouse they were at was Celia's and it was used as a receiving station for Cutta. How stupid could they have been to kill this fool there!

"You guys are some stupid idiots, that's Cutta's place, so why would you kill him there?"

"Kill Cutta, what you talking about primo, I only wish. We got his sister!"

My heart dropped! It was like I was in the twilight zone. I would have killed Queen to save my family but only as a last alternative. If anyone was going to end her life it was going to be me! I shook Celia from her rest and told her what had just happened. She immediately jumped up and we were on our way to the warehouse still in our night ware. Once we arrived at the warehouse, I saw my worst nightmare! It was Queen wrapped in separate garbage bags like she was nothing worth loving! I was outraged! I looked at Solo and he just smirked and said,

"I guess you have to get another BTCH now!"

Time began to slow. Everything sounded like Charlie Brown's parents talking to him over the phone. Sosa was in the corner cleaning the blood off of his self and then it happened. I pulled my gun and shot Solo in the head. Sosa rushed over to his dropping body and as I was about to put one in him, Celia jumped in his path.

"Baker what the hell is your problem! That is your cousin, he's family primo!"

I couldn't hear her! All I saw was the ones who took away the only female I truly loved! With a clam voice I ordered Celia to move! Revenge was all I had on my mind, and I was going to stop at nothing to proceed.

"Move Celia." I said calmly

"Or what primo, you gone kill me too?"

"If I have to."

By that time Sosa's tears were drying and his anger was rising.

"You killed my brother you sick FCK!"

Celia was in my face and wouldn't get out of the path of my gun. I heard two shots and she dropped like a bag of bricks. Sosa was shooting like a mad man. I ran ducked behind one of the pallets on the floor full of building supplies. I shot back two times and waited for him to empty his gun. I heard a click and that's when I made my move. I jumped up and fired two more shots in his direction. As he tried to run away one hit him in his back. He fell down, stumbling and rolling trying hard to get up. I went over to him, took my foot and put it on his back. I then rolled him over and told him to look at me. When he looked up I fired a single shot in his head and ran back over to Celia. She was gargling blood and couldn't talk. I panicked. I didn't know what to do. I picked her up and dragged her to the warehouse elevator but by the time I got her there I could hear her take her last breath. I was sick.

I ran to the car and dashed out of there as quick as I could. Where did it all go so wrong? Not only Queen was dead, but my Celia also. I got back to the house and cleaned up. I placed my old bloody clothes in garbage bag and took them to an alleyway near the house and burned them. I sat in the house after that lethargic, but I knew I had to pull myself together or a windstorm was about to happen. I guess what made me a ruthless, successful killer was the fact I could deny my feelings at the drop of a dime to conceal my actions.

The next day, the news had hit the streets like a ball of fire! I knew Cutta had no choice but to resurface now. I also knew I was safe because Celia, Sosa and Solo were dead too. It didn't make me look suspicious. Now all I had to do was keep my game face on when I went to Queen's funeral because running into Cutta was now definitely without question!

Once the news had got back to Virginia, Sammy and Grand were on the next flight to the city. The whole crew even came. Celia's funeral was first. When Cutta showed up you could tell it was hitting him hard. I had never seen him in that state. He was distraught. His tears flowed like waterfalls. I was numb. It was the only way I could keep my composure.

"I know I haven't been around youth, but I'm back and I got your back on this because I know what you want to do!"

He was clueless just like I needed everyone to be.

"I know Cutta, it's on now!"

He just shook his head in agreement.

"We'll meet later after Queen's funeral and talk. I also have a big shipment I need you to pick up from Panama once you get back home. I think it's time to step you youths up to the big time."

Queen's funeral was beautiful. Cutta stopped at nothing to make sure her home going service was one to remember. It didn't help my conscious but I didn't let it affect me neither. After her funeral we all went back to the funeral home and had a meeting with Cutta. He said that he had a new connect and everything was now going to be bigger than ever before. The truth was starting to unfold. Panama seemed to be right.

We all wanted to stay for a while but Cutta wanted us to go back to Virginia to handle the business and get the streets back in order. My plans for Cutta were halted for the time being, and I had no clue what was about to unfold next.

Baker Grimes
Hamza Atoi
CHAPTER ELEVEN

The murder of Celia and Queen had to have been the worst points in my life. It took me a very long time to get over it and it surely changed the direction my life took. Normally things of that nature would change you in a good way but for me it was the opposite. The incidents in New York made me careless. I often said to myself over and over again this life was not for us, but something kept us drawn in. It couldn't have been the money because by that time we were caked up. What was it? I'd like to say it was destiny but truly we all have the choice to make destiny do as we wish. Why I allowed her to dictate my life I have no idea. The one thing I knew was this, destiny had her hooks me like an O'Jays song.

In my lifestyle I had no time for weakness. If anyone saw that flaw you were soon to be on the chopping block with either no work or no life! I had to pull it all together because Cutta gave word to meet with Panama to pick up a shipment.

Fame and I made the pickup. This time he had more security than normal and it shook Fame and I for a minute. We were wondering if he was setting us up. We had a bag full of money to exchange for the work.

"So what up P? What's the extra manpower for?"

"Bigger shipment, more manpower." He said with a Donald Trump business tone. He pointed to the two duffle bags. They looked extremely larger than normal. I heard a rumor Panama loved to cut up people and put them in duffle bags so I was very hesitant to look in them at first.

"Is there a problem my friend?"

"You tell me?" Why all the extra work?"

"Your boss hit the big time, you didn't know?" I didn't know anything. We once were pushing three kilos at a time and in those bags we counted 24. I didn't think we could handle that much weight but before I could say anything else Fame picked up both the bags and began to walk to the warehouse door.

"So Baker I'll get with you later?" I nodded my head and followed Fame back to the car. What was Cutta trying to do? I didn't want to be a part of another scheme and I definitely didn't want to be set up or watched by the Feds. Why did he trust us with that much weight? I had no clue.

Fame and I got back to the spot out Park Place and showed the Noize Makers what we were now pushing. We had 24 kilos of pure, uncut Panamanian cocaine. Cutta gave us a good profit margin on each and that instantly put us in another money bracket. We all split the bricks up and everyone begin to create their own clientele. We had only one rule. Every client had to be disclosed to each Noize Maker so we could keep tabs on each other and rule out one another if the client seemed shady. Like always we all agreed to the rule and everyone grabbed their product and we went their separate ways.

We continued to move heavy weight. The school year was coming to a close and Sammy Hawk and Clarkboy were graduating so Panama decided to give them a party. He rented out this club in Downtown Norfolk called "Pizzazz" owned by this dude named "Black." Black use to be a big time enforcer himself before doing time Fed time. When he came out he took all of his money and went legit. They use to call him "Beetle juice" because if his name was heard more than three times in a conversation you were destined to meet him. Black was a cool dude. When we got to the club he had bottles of Moet waiting for us at a private table on the second floor. We were all dressed in suit jackets and pants. Our feet were dipped in suede Bally boots. We were being treating like royalty.

I had a chance to sit down and talk to Black for a while. He told me how things use to be and said he heard about us running the streets. Black had a good outlook on life and tried hard to lead me in the right direction. Out of all the people who ever tried to school me, he was the one I really listened to. He knew the streets better than anyone I had known and knew the outcome of them also. I sat there and continued to talk with Black while everyone else enjoyed the night's festivities. He told me I could try and stack up all the money I wanted and that still wouldn't ensure I would make it out alive or out of chains. I said to myself, "If an ex killer as ruthless as the stories go about him could change, than so could a kid like me." Who was I fooling?" What Black schooled me on was true but how was I going to get out of a life that was now bigger than me?

Black and I chilled together for most of the night until Daja walked in. I was surprised to see her and really didn't expect her to come. She was dressed sexy as ever. She had on this little tight fitting dress and her jewels were flawless.

"So you gone get me a drink NGHA?"

Black just laughed and moved over in the booth to make room for her and her friends. She was trying to shine on me. I paid her no mind, got her a glass of Moet and sat her down beside us. I introduced her to Black and he immediately cut me the eye. I looked over his shoulder and two girls in the distance were standing at the end of the bar staring at us. I told Daja to go and get her something to eat and drink. Black gave her a VIP card that entitled her to free drinks and food and they were off. Black told me they had been staring for a while so I went to see who it was. To my surprise it was Sarah.

She had talked with Sammy and he invited her without asking me or even having the foresight to imagine if Daja might show up. I kept it cool because Sarah knew the deal but Daja was a live wire. If she had an idea something was going on with Sarah and I she would have turned that club out. I went back over to the table and told Black what was going on and he took me to a private suite on the third floor so I could be alone with Sarah.

It was good seeing her again because we only talked over the phone since we left the program.

"It's good to see you Baker. I thought you only like my voice for a while."

"No it's not like that. I've just been busy.

"So, was that Daja?"

"Yeah that's her." She told me she thought she was fly and I picked right because she would never be as fly as her. I told her she was wrong. I told her Daja was loud with her style. She had to be in the spotlight to be seen and she was just right. She smiled and grabbed me by my face and kissed me. She began to take off my suit coat and kiss me. Our kisses lead to our first time.

Sarah smelled like a bushel of roses. With each kiss I could feel her back arch like a bow. Once we were finished we smiled at each other and placed our clothes back on to go downstairs. Before I could get out of the door Black was running in telling me to stay put because Daja was drunk and looking all over for me. He said she was throwing drinks on security and blabbing out I was a killer and if any one touched her she was going to have them in dirt by the morning. Black went back down and told me he was going to handle the situation personally. He had a way with women, but I said to myself, "Daja is not your ordinary chick."

He came back up and said the coast was clear. He was laughing harder than a hyena. He got one of his boys to take Daja and her girls' home and gave them all a thousand dollars and said it was from me. He told them I had to leave and to use the money to go to the mall the next day. Daja was money hungry so his plan worked without flaw. I pulled out three thousand dollars from my pocket and tried to pay him back the money he gave them. He said I was insulting him and told me considerate a love gesture for our new friendship. Black was one of the realest dudes I had met. He was one of the only ones who didn't want anything in return for what he did. We parted ways that night but I kept in touch with him. I was glad I did because later down the line his friendship ended up saving my life.

Things began to change with Cutta and I. We started to talk more. When I called him he would always answer in a day or two. It put me on alert because he never called back so frequently before. Sammy felt he was calling a lot because of all the work we were pushing by ourselves. Since we did in his two men he had working for us only protection we had was our own. Not to say that was a bad thing because we were surly skilled in street warfare, but we were still young. Hush came down every now and then to check on us. I never said anything to him about what Panama said. I wanted to see if he would tell me first. He didn't. Hush was as calculated as they came. He never spoke too much or out of turn. He only told you what needed to be said.

Before the start of my senior year I received news that was haunting. Daja was pregnant. She was the last girl I needed carrying my kid but it was too late for all that then. I wasn't raised to duck out on my responsibility so it was now time to grow up and handle real business. I can't front. I tried to get her to get an abortion. I didn't want my child to have to deal with the lost of my life or me locked up. I also knew people loved to use your family to get information from you.

A seed would put my lifestyle at risk and would have to be extra careful of the way I moved. I think she took it harder than I did but she couldn't see herself disposing her child for any reason.

I thought when I told my grandmother she would flip out. Surprisingly she was very happy. She didn't like the fact it was out of wedlock but the fact a child was on the way excited her. Sammy thought it was a bad move and often told me I messed up. Black told me the best thing was to continue school and graduate, and go to ODU and get my bachelors in Journalism like I dreamed of. He said that was a good way to leave that life behind me. It sounded good but would it really happen?

Daja was already a sore in the flesh of my business and now it was going to be worst. I don't know why I didn't let her go from the jump. This was one of the many bad decisions I made. I was going to have to keep her happy so she wouldn't be vindictive. She had a little insight on what I did but never really knew how in depth my business went. It didn't matter because in this commonwealth state all you needed to bring someone down was insight. Killing her was out of the question if she became out of hand. How do you kill the mother of your kids? It was something I wasn't going to ever do. Instead of making a situation bad, I made the best out of it. I spoiled her. I gave her anything she wanted and that made her happy. I also didn't want her stressing while carrying our child. Instead of going to school I paid for her to home school. Sometimes it was a problem because she was the type that had to be seen. I just kept the gifts coming. It wasn't time to let up. We went to the doctor and found out we were having a boy. She said she wanted to name him after me but I was against it. I never said anything to her but I just kept giving her alternates. My name I felt was the reason I was destined into this madness, and I wasn't about to let him be named after me, but of course her bickering won the case.

I bought Little Baker everything before he was even born. He was going to have the best. I put money aside for college and even had a trust fund set up that not even his mother could touch. I was making plans for him and not allowing destiny to do it for me.

I remember the night of his birth. Daja called me about two in the morning. She was terrified. She said her water broke and was panicking. I was with Panama at the time and we both dashed over to Norfolk General. When I got there, her Grandfather said they took her in the back because she had dilated 10 centimeters and was ready to push. Man! Let me tell you something! Killing people never made me sick or nauseas, but seeing my child born was different. I was holding her hand as she squeezed mine with the power of a silver back gorilla. I didn't know how to help or soothe her. I handled my business like I was an adult but handled the birth of my son like the teenager I was. His head popped out. I swear to you homie, I don't remember the rest. All I remember is Daja holding my beautiful son and laughing at me as I gained consciousness. We laughed the entire night and our relationship seemed ordinary for a change. In spite of our shortcomings, Daja was my girl and now the mother of my son

The birth of my son didn't stop me from graduating from high school. It was now Tony and my turn to walk across the stage. My grandmother was once again proud of me. Everyone who was close to me was in attendance. Surprisingly Cutta even came. Panama, Black and Dr. Shakur were also in attendance. The one thing I wasn't expecting walked through the door and my attention of holding a high school diploma was diverted. It was Swampman! He was out of jail. From the back of the auditorium I could see his pearl white teeth breech the lips of his dark round face. I wanted to jump off the stage and run to him but I held my composure. The Noize Makers were now one man stronger. It was time to party but not because of my accomplishment. One of our original Noize members was home and we wanted to show him what corner store money had now turned into.

This time Black threw a big celebration for Tony and I. Everyone was in attendance. Cutta showered me with money and gifts and Black gave me a twenty thousand dollar scholarship from a foundation he started for inner city youth. Panama had the Moet flowing like a river and all was well for a change. Swampman was still his old self. He hit the dance floor like he was on Soul Train. We were having a ball. We sat at our VIP table and filled him in on what was going on in Park Place. He wasn't shocked to hear news of us running the streets. He said he was given special favors in jail because people knew he was with us.

"The streets know who we are Bake! I lived like a king in that jank! Everyone was afraid to touch me even the corrections officers."

I was happy to hear he survived the experience with minor setbacks. We all gave him ten thousand dollars each to get him back on his feet. In that time period he had lost not only his mom but also his grandmother who was his biggest support system. He stayed with Sammy and Aunt Marisa for a while until Sammy, Hawk and he got their own condo at Newpointe in Virginia Beach. He didn't hit the work force until Sammy schooled him on the way the streets were now operating. When he went in he was only 13 years old. It had been five years since that awful day, and a lot had changed on those blocks since then.

Baker Grimes
Hamza Atoi
CHAPTER TWELVE

Time was pushing on and everything was running normal. We continued to move work and slowly indoctrinated Swampman back in. I remember the call from Cutta when the tides changed direction on us. He told me he needed me to take a trip to New York and talk with him in person. I told him the Noize Makers and I were planning a trip there in a couple weeks and I would see him then. He insisted I come alone because the business didn't involve them only me. I wasn't about to go to New York alone with all the incidents that had transpired over the years. Sammy said he felt like it was a set up but that had to have been far from the truth. If he wanted to reach out to me he had the money and manpower to have it done here. It didn't make sense but I had to go.

I took a separate flight from everyone else. He must have been out of his mind to really think they would stay home. Fame was the only one who didn't come but he couldn't because of other obligations to Panama. We got with Uncle Flip and he hooked us up with an arsenal in case it hit the fan. He even had some old time players on standby if we needed them. Uncle never trusted Cutta and neither did I.

I gave him a call a day later and told him to meet me at his restaurant in Queens but he had another location in mind. He wanted me to meet him at the warehouse across the street from where Queen, Celia, Sosa and Solo were murdered. He had something up his sleeve and he knew if I backed out I did also. I could tell he was trying to extract information from me. He was never going to let the death of Queen go unanswered. Noize and I came up with a plan. Sammy and Hawk followed me to the meeting. Swampman and Tony were already there on the building across the street. If I knew Cutta correctly he was going to pick the space facing the window where Queen met her demise. He did that exactly. I knew what this meeting was all about. He was ready to put Queen's murder to rest. I walked in the warehouse and two of his boys immediately walked up to me and tried to frisk me for guns. I pulled out before they could put their hands on me and said,

"If you're worried about me being strapped, do these answer your question?" Cutta motioned to his men to stand down and giggled, "You always been on top of your game Bake." I wasn't about to let this dude catch me slipping.

"So why the New York meet and greet? It's obviously a problem somewhere, so let's get to it!" I kept my two P-90 Rugers off safety ready for whatever was to come next.

"No problem I hope?" He started to grill me again about the night they were murdered. He said he had a lot of ground he wanted to cover and the phones were no longer safe. I was a good liar and had an even better memory so his efforts to confuse me were useless. I told him everything I told him before. What he couldn't figure out was why Celia was there and not I? He knew we were playing chess that night so why did she rush to the warehouse when the brothers called and not I?

"You and your cousin hung tight before then so why the separation Grimy?"

"Celia was a big girl homie. She didn't need me to go everywhere with her. Trust me if I was with her she and Queen would be here Right now!"

"Your two cousins wouldn't? What? Did you three have beef?" He knew something and I had no time to figure it out. I wondered did Queen talk to him after all? The questions he asked fit the situation too perfect. I told him when he had some news about the killings to hit me up. I turned my back and started walking away. I knew he wouldn't kill me there. It was also a gesture to show him I wasn't scared. He yelled as I was leaving, "I'll see you before you leave alright Bake? I'll take you the restaurant, I know you like that?" I turned around guns still drawn and smiled. I think he knew. Why he wasn't trying to kill me or get the real information by torturing me was a mystery. I knew now he would be on alert. I should have listened to Panama. I had to come up with a way to get at him before he got us.

The rest of the Noize makers were ready to let him have it that night. Uncle flip told us we had to be patient and put the pieces to the puzzle together. He was more than sure that Cutta killed his Celia. My acting continued flawless because no one knew I did it besides Sammy. We spent a week in New York soaking up the nightlife. Destiny at that time was still in love with me. She gave me the gift I had been waiting for in the form of an old memory. She gave me Oshun.

Tony and I were visiting some old clients we knew on 149th and Saint Nicholas. She pulled up shining in a new Pink Jetta with pink and gold rims. She must have hit a lick because the last time I saw her she was as broke as abandon building windows in the projects. She didn't see me at first. She jumped out the whip jewels shining and body more banging than when I first met her. She and I both had grown since the last time we saw each other. She was on her cell phone when I came up from behind her and felt that fat old booty. She jumped back ready to slap the hell out of whoever did it and saw that it was me. I didn't get the reaction I thought I was going to get instead she jumped in my arms and started kissing me like I was her man.

"Oh snap...Baker? I really missed you! How long has it been?"

"I've been in and out of New York mama but haven't seen you since...well you know...that was a sad time for both of us." She lowered her head for a second and asked how Sammy was doing. I told him he was fine and is in New York also. She said she heard about what happen to Queen and Celia.

"I had to get out of here Baker after Oshun was murdered. I live in Philly now. I do choreography for all the big time rappers."

"Yo! That's caliente! It's always good to get away from this life." She asked how I was doing. It was obvious by my jewels and gear I was still getting money.

"Everything is everything...how y'all say it up here...ya mean!" She smiled and we continued our conversation as if nothing ever happened. Panama said Asia and Oshun was in on it but if Oshun was still living she could not have possibly known the deal was going to be a robbery. She told me she wanted to meet up with me later to take me out to dinner. My favorite spot in New York was "Sylvia's" so I told her to take me there. I was kind of happy to see her so I told her it would be even better if we hung out for the rest of the day. She was with it. Oshun was now making money. The first New York trip she was Miss Gold digger. That wasn't the case anymore. We went shopping in New York's diamond district and other hot spots and not once did she ask me for cheddar. She was paying everything dolo. She even bought me this dope diamond pinky ring. She said her dad was a real New York player at one time and all of their crew wore pinky rings. I already had a banging iced out bracelet so my left hand was now upgraded.

Dinner at Sylvia's was going great until the mood changed from good time to a police questioning.

"Hey Baker. Why did you go back to Virginia so fast after Asia was murdered?" My face went blank. This was a conversation I didn't want to have but I knew would come up.

"Everything here was out of control. My grandmother wanted us back in V.A. immediately. We didn't know what was going on. Some people said it was a hit."

I didn't want to talk anymore. It was something her eyes that looked like the Asia of old. She just stared at me for a minute and then smiled.

"Let's not ruin the moment with all the bad history. You want to go to my room?" I wanted to go because that backside was calling me but I had always been paranoid. I suspected everything was a set up after what happen to Sammy and Fire. I declined.

"Maybe another time, I really have to get back to Brooklyn."

Her face changed just as I expected. It was a set up. All of a sudden she shows up in Harlem…yeah right. I didn't know if I needed to call a cab or just allow her to take me home. I didn't want to tip her off. I told her I would be back I had to go to the bathroom. I left the table looking back as I was walking away. She instantly got on the phone. It was a hit! I went to the waiter and asked was there another way out. I gave a 100-dollar bill and he took me through the back and I was off. I knew it was too good to be true. As I jetted trying to hail a cab, I seen this all black Jetta pull up and it was my old clients from 149th. They were all in on it. I remember one dude I had never seen before eyeballing me the entire time. I kept my peripherals on him and continued my conversation.

Harlem was always known for its tact with setting up a sting. They were real smooth with it. They weren't like Brooklynites who would just run up on you and bang you with the heat then be out with the dough. I was on foreign turf. It wasn't like back home. New York was a do for your self-type of city. They were neighborhood tight. Even though I had mad clout there, I was an outsider. As I made my move trying to get a cab destiny sent me a favor, it was Hush.

"Baker! What you doing out here by yourself son...man if you don't get in this whip kid!" I was so happy to see him. I told him what was going on and to circle back around so I could see if they were indeed with Oshun. We drove back past Sylvia's and like I thought. Asia was standing by their car like she was puzzled.

"Yo Oshun tried to set me up!" Hush looked at me shaking his head. He always thought I had the better judgment out of the crew but that proved otherwise.

"Tony told me you left him in Harlem with Scottie and trick. Trick never did like you and was always plotting to get you. He just never did because Cutta and me."

"So why is he trying now?" Hush's eyes looked dim.

"Word on the street, Cutta and the Noize Makers are splitting ways. You and the crew are on your own now kid, and the wolves are out." Why would Cutta cut us off like that? He didn't have any evidence of what happen.

"So why are you here big homie?" I asked with a concerned voice because if we were out then so was Hush's protection.

"I'm here for Celia. She wouldn't want me to let anything happen to you guys." I didn't understand. Why would he being doing it for Celia?

We got back to Uncle Flip's and set in front of the Brownstone and he told me what I never expected.

"Celia and I use to be something. That's why Cutta and I had beef once. He pushed up on her after I got locked for a hit I did for him. When I got out they were together. I ran up on him not thinking he was with security and one of them hit me with a razor." He continued on about how much he loved her but never once showed any emotion. He was hardcore. His feelings were as hidden as a catholic schoolteachers smile.

"I didn't know big homie." I could tell he really loved her. He then cut the conversation short and said we had to kill Cutta and we had to do it quick. I was with it but it was no real way to get close to him. He had his security on him like he was the president. Hush wasn't sure if Cutta was going to kill us then but he said he would eventually send someone. It was time to get out of New York. We had a better chance at fighting him on our turf.

Baker Grimes
Hamza Atoi
CHAPTER THIRTEEN

A simple game of Atari and Coleco Vision had now turned into a deadly empire. We were in deep and now it had dire consequences. We weren't kids anymore, and high school was over. It was real world time.

I never told the Noize Makers about Cutta's plan because I didn't want anyone to freak out and do something stupid. The block was getting more outrageous and we had to shut down a lot of street corner operations because we didn't want any work to lead back to us. We went from moving half and whole bricks to breaking a lot of it down because Tony had a big street clientele. It was a risky move but in that life you had to take some chances. We didn't want the streets to become bigger than our crew so we did what we had to do to solidify our superiority. It was now to a point were hiding was totally out of the question. The Feds were eventually going to be on us so we knew it was time to move the whole organization out of Virginia. We had some trusted school friends we put down. They knew what they had got themselves into so if they were caught they were on their own.

Fame hadn't been checking in like he was suppose to after we got back from New York. He would be missing for months and then just show up with the cash he owed. He would then pick up his next duffle bag of work and be out. I didn't like it at all. We had mandatory meetings once a week and he would show up for only one. This was a corporation in our eyes. If he wasn't going to abide by the by laws he was going to be voted out. I took it to Noize to see how they felt about it but they didn't agree.

They knew Fame was moving a good amount of weight out of town and that was fine with them. As long as we had the money to pay Cutta they were cool.

Cutta was still giving us large amounts of weight in spite of what Hush said. I knew Hush wouldn't lie so I made moves to set up another connect just in case he bucked on us. I started out getting us ten kilos at the start. I didn't want to move too much because we continued moving the twenty bricks for Cutta also. I used a hook up in Miami with some Zoe Boys I knew. They were on some real live pirate SHT and were hitting all the Columbian and Cubano boats. They were coming off like a fat cat so I threw a lot of money their way. It was also a business move because when in Miami moving product you didn't want them on your track. They also knew every move someone from out of town made in their territory, which helped me with a Noize member in particular, Fame.

Sammy and I made a business trip to Carol City for a gun shipment a Zoe named Grimmo had. We were making our arsenal stronger because we were soon going to go to war with Cutta. Grimmo had a link with his cousin who was an ATF agent. He would sell Grimmo stockpiles of supposedly destroyed weapons and Grimmo made a killing off of them. While waiting for the shipment to be pulled around he asked us if we were still cool with Fame. Sammy and I looked Puzzled because minus his absences at the meetings we had no problem with him.

"Why you ask that Grimmo?"

"It's none of my business but he said that you all were on the way out." It was strange but not out of the question to hear of Fame doing deals away from the Noize Makers. We knew he was going to sooner or later cut out but we thought it would still be some loyalty. The way Grimmo gave us the information; he was ready for war if needed. Sammy and I were pissed.

"I'm not trying bring up a war but you two do a lot of business with me and I just don't want to be in the middle of something that would have us all using these weapons on each other if you see where I'm coming from."

I understood fully. We were stockpiling guns, readying ourselves for a war. I remember hearing rumors that Lee-Lee was now pushing a little work on the high-end side of the street level himself. The only way that was going to happen was if Fame had supplied him because Fame had Huntersville on lock. No one was pushing anything without his approval. I now had a lot of love for Fame so I felt more than betrayed. Grimmo had no reason to lie because a war would be costly for us all. We told him we would keep the conversation silent. Grimmo was a lot cooler with us than Fame. With Fame it was business but with us it was a little more because Grimmo was going out with our cousin that lived in Coconut Grove.

When Sammy and I got back to Norfolk we decided to keep that part of the conversation hidden from Noize like I decided to keep Cutta's arrangements to myself. Sammy was trying to keep me cool because he knew what I wanted to do. I told him I would chill for now but I had to find out if the stories about Lee-Lee were true. It would be a vital piece to the puzzle of truth about Fame.

It was a Friday night and I decided to go out with the Noize Makers and have some fun. Swampman, Tony, and our security team went with me. We went to this poppin' spot in Virginia Beach Called Mr. Magic's. All of the some bodies went there to club alongside all the gold diggers and stick up kids. It was a spot that we had mad respect in with all the big wheels because most of them we supplied. I always had the mentality to keep drinking to a minimum because I never liked being tore down when I was out in public. Mr. Magic's was famous for its Twenty-dollar craft drinks. Tony and Swampman were wasted. It was this big vase like container and one of those from the right bartender would have you done. Our security was always on point and never drunk anything when we went out.

My number one bodyguard in particular, was Neevak. He was a pretty boy and always had the ladies going crazy. I met Neevak at the basketball court on Ballentine Boulevard in Norfolk. I was waiting to play a pickup game and this dude from

Bowling Park jumped in my face saying he was next in line. I played it cool because it was no reason to get in beef over a basketball game but he was on a stunt mission. I gave him the ball and told him he was had it and I went to sit on the Bench when he tried to sneak me from behind. I truly didn't see it coming and almost got knocked until Neevak snuffed the dude out with one punch. Homie was sleeping like a baby. Neevak then runs across the street and comes back with this humongous pit bull. The court cleared like Florida skies after a rainstorm. I was standing by the street and yelled to him it was cool because he was about to let this dog go bananas on the guy. He looked up and laughed. He ran the dog back across the street came back and I got us out of there. I didn't know much about him at first. All I knew was he was a star football player at our school and the women loved him. I later found out from a couple killers out Ballentine that Neevak was nuts. They said he was one of the most feared in Norfolk and that kind of dude I needed on my team.

Like I said before, we all went out and was having a good time. I looked across the floor and I see Neevak in the cut with his gun by his side. All I was thinking was I know he isn't about to bang anyone. He never made a move without consulting with me so it had to have been something for him to be in that position. He walked back over to me and grabs me by my arm and slowly walked me out of the club. The rest of our team grabbed Swampman and Tony. We all jumped in our vehicles and Neevak grabs the sawed off shotgun he had by the seat.

"Yo! What's going on Neevak?" He told me he saw Lee-Lee in the corner eyeballing me. One of the dudes he had with him had his gun out. I was slipping because I didn't even see Lee-Lee come in the club. I asked him how was he dressed and Neevak said that he was flossing big time. He had a stack of money and was even accompanied by one of Fame's security. In my eyes the whole entire story was true. I didn't need any more evidence than that.

It was time to put an end to the beef with Lee-Lee before it messed up business. I remember one time Fame saying Lee- Lee was a hot head. He told Fame if the police ever ran up on him he wasn't going to jail. Lee-Lee was the type of dude that had to prove a point because no one ever paid him any mind. He was nobody! I learned from him *nobodies* are the most dangerous people you could will deal with in the game. *Nobodies* wanted to be *somebodies* and would do whatever to get the rep.

Lee-Lee was known as the dirty kid from the village. He wore no name brand shoes and one pair of jeans five days a week. The only reason Fame put him on because he never liked anyone picking with the underdog. He took Lee under his wing and it got to a point where he thought he was on the same level as Fame. Fame knew he could cause trouble at the wrong time but that was his boy. I knew Fame had some hard feelings about us stomping Lee out but tried to squash it because of business. What he was telling me now was business in his eyes was down and forget Noize!

I knew I couldn't touch Fame but Lee was another story. I sent Neevak to watch him for about two weeks to see what his routine was. Neevak reported back and said he had C Avenue jumping. He said they were set up in a house with runners and a lookout. I knew whatever I did to get him was going to have to be creative and far away from my hands.

I had never been an advocate for snitching but the idea I came up with was the only way to hit him without actually doing the work myself. I called the Detectives at the Norfolk Police Department and told them about the spot. I even told them they were heavily armed and one dude in particular was a cop killer. A couple months before two crooked cops where murdered for shaking people down for money. It wasn't our crew who did it so don't ask! People just got tired of their raw deals so I guess death was the only way. Let me get back to the story.

No one knew they were on the take so when they were hit, it came with a windstorm. All of the cops were still pissed about their fellow comrade's murder. It was the best I could come up with to keep the trail away from us. If Lee-Lee were hit any other way, Fame would have suspected me even if it weren't.

The cops raided Lee-Lee's spot faster than I expected. It had only been two days since I made the anonymous call from a phone booth. Destiny was playing fare for a change. It went down just like Fame said Lee wanted to go out. The streets said Lee was on the balcony when the cops pulled up and started bussing an AK-47 before they could even get out the car. It was a war on C Avenue and by the time it ended, two more cops were dead as well as everyone in the house; including Lee-Lee.

Neevak said they had the block jumping which meant majority of the product inside was ours. Fame was now out of a well-oiled machine in Huntersville. We knew he wasn't going to tell us but the money would. If the spot was off the hook like Neevak said his pockets took a major hit.

All of a sudden Fame started attending more meetings. He asked for an extension on part of his dough and that let Sammy and I know it was his spot Lee was operating. The cops had found guns, and two bricks of broke down product in the raid. We didn't know how we would handle the situation. Sammy didn't want him dead but if need be it was going to happen. Fame had been a Noize maker from almost the start. He was my hanging partner for a while until he started sexing my girl. Yeah homie, Fame was hitting Daja off behind my back.

Remember the story I was telling you about when we all went to the movies? It all started there. Fame was with her, chilling like she wasn't my girl when I was in New York dealing with that nonsense from Cutta. He said he was staying back to put in work with Panama but when I talked to Panama that weekend he said he hadn't seen Fame. I let it roll on for a minute until I had enough. With all of the rumors going around it only enhanced my anger.

It was Fame's 20th birthday. He was never the partying type so we just had a little something for him over Sammy and Swampman's spot. All of our girls were there. I didn't want Daja with me but I knew of course she would have been a real pain so I gave her some money to go shopping for the night. When I went to pick her up she was dressed like a stripper.

"Where you think you going with that on?"

"You ain't my Daddy! Anyway I wanted to look fly for tonight. Is that ok with you?"

"We are only going to Sammy's crib for a Noize get together not the club Daja." She just rolled her eyes and sat quite in the car humming Lil Kim's song "F NGHAS get money."

We got to Sammy's condo and he had it laid out for Fame. He had shrimp, lobster, steak and Moet on the table. Fame came in with one of his girls from the village. She was banging! Her backside was thick like two country hams were in her jeans. Daja was on her hate game. She was trying to hold it in but it showed like a black light on bloodstains. We were all having a blast. Daja was quite on the couch and I could tell she had an attitude. Fame's girl was all over him as we toasted his big day then Daja just jumped up and went in the bathroom and stayed there for a minute. We were all engaging in a conversation when I noticed she was gone. I went to the bathroom and it looked like her makeup was fresh. Her eyes were red and she was sniffling.

"What's wrong with you?" I said with an angry tone."

"I want to go home I'm bored!" She was the one who was pushing Sammy to ask me if she could go. Now all of a sudden she was bored?

"I'm not ready to leave yet, just chill and mingle. Chill out with Fame's girl she seems cool." Daja's facial expression had changed. I knew I struck a button.

"I don't know that BTCH, what I want to talk with her for?" Daja was moving her neck in that angry black women motion. She was heated.

"Well, I'm not going home; you do what you want to!" I walked out calm but inside I was heated. I knew she was mad because Fame had another broad there. She thought she was going to floss in front him and me not know it. She thought I was stupid.

The night was finally coming to an end and everyone was drunk. Sammy told us all to stay or call someone from the security team to take us home. I was about to call Neevak until Fame and his girl said they were going to stay. Daja then change from rude to joyful and said we might as well stay also. She called her sister and told her she was going to stay out for the rest of the night and I told her I would give her a thousand dollars for watching little Bake for us. We stayed up for a while playing spades while the girls finally had an estrogen session.

Daja was now acting like the girl was a best friend. She was up to something. I wasn't a dummy. I knew she was sick the entire night because Fame had another girl at the get together. Jealousy was starting to sink in but I didn't show it. With every smile Fame made Daja gaze even harder. Sammy looked at me because he even saw what was going on. I just nodded at him to show, I was cool. He knew something was brewing inside me. The older I became in age the more Sammy had seen my rage grow.

The life we had come accustom to was consuming us all in its own way. It was strange to see us all in one place away from the normal activities kids our age missed out on. We were local drug kingpins and killers. Each man in the room was easily worth about two hundred grand or better. That was a lot of money for age. Destiny set us up with a choice that led in the same direction no matter which one we chose.

The morning had arrived and everyone was scattered all over the condo. I awoke first and what I saw fueled my anger and moved it into a deadly overdrive. Daja was on the couch with Fame in the middle of him and his girl. I didn't want to cause a scene so I just got up and left. I told Sammy before I dipped to call a cab for Daja and tell her I would get with her later. On my way home I was heated. Each thought had me ready to do damage. It was time for Fame to die.

Fame's death was personal. He had cross the line too many times. He was playing us like our crew wasn't deadly. His arrogance placed him in the position he is in now, face up and six feet deep.

The night of his murder wasn't out of the ordinary. We had just finished a meeting, which he was now attending on a regular basis. He asked if I wanted to hang and it instantly became the opportunity I needed.

We bought two Forties of Old English and sat in the city Park and reminisced about the younger days when money wasn't a factor. It was fun to have but friends were more important.

"Life is too serious now Baker." He said while passing a freshly rolled Philly packed with hydroponic weed. We were getting high and blasted out of our mind. I then slipped up. That was why I never liked to drink much because I was and angry drunk.

"Why you sticking my girl Fame?" He looked at me and put down his forty. He had this smirk on his face like he was caught but he wouldn't own up to it. Fame knew if he told me I would have killed him before he could finish his sentence.

"You're bugging NGHA. Why would I stick Daja? She ain't even my type." His words were very nonchalant. It was starting to piss me off more.

"Baker just smoke this and shut the hell up!" He said with an assured giggle that I was cool and all was well. I just stared at him. He knew that look because he had seen it when he first met me.

"So this is where it's going to happen Baker? Right here? Right now?" He started running and reaching for his gun. I gave chase and was struggling to get mine gun out also. He tripped over one of the protruding tree roots from City Park's vase array of greenery. I shot twice hitting him in the chest. Fame always wore a vest so I knew the shots only stung him. I stood over him and asked him the same question again. Once again he denied it.

"I didn't stick your girl homie, but if you don't kill me now, I'm going to stick her good and then I'm going to kill you!" He said with grunting pains he received from my 45 Cal.

"Wrong answer Fame! I loved you homie! I'm sorry!" I fired two shots in his head and ran back to my car and drove off like nothing ever happened.

The staff of Parks and Recreation found his body. The news about Fame was big media coverage locally and abroad. Fame was being investigated. That was the word we got from one of our insiders with Norfolk Police Department. The murder paid off. I thought it wouldn't hit me but his murder did. At that time I wished I could turn back the hands of history and bring back all those who were gone because of our stupidity and greed. We had many chances to get out but the big lights and popularity had us veiled from the reality of this moment. Hustling and killing only leads to your own eventual death. Many say they wish they had what we had. I say this to them. If they only knew what we had been through to achieve our so-called success they would change their mind and run to the nearest church.

Fame's funeral was laid out. I felt like Bishop from the movie "Juice." I was standing there like nothing ever happened. I knew it was going to come to this one way or another. It was either he or we and I wanted to live! You can call it jealousy but who really gives a FCK what you think!

Baker Grimes
Hamza Atoi
CHAPTER FOURTEEN

It had been weeks since Fame's death and I felt like it was all coming to an end. Life was starting to give me this eerie feeling. It looked as if everything resembled death. I walked the streets more paranoid than ever. It was hard to even take my son to the park because I felt like everyone was looking at me. I went to the mall and it was as if its occupants knew I killed Fame. I needed to get away but if I left too soon I would have the streets, and the cops, who now knew who we were, buzzing. The cops knew our status in Park Place because it was no longer a secret, but we stilled played the dumb kid roll. Catching us wasn't going to be easy. We had a lot of their officers on our pay roll. Our only concern was their true loyalty.

I remember the first time a cop ever ran up on me. I was standing on the corner of 35th and Newport avenue in front of Mr. Green's after hour's spot called "Thorns." I was eating a pork chop sandwich and fries just chilling with some old friends from around the way and this crazy cop named Arnold pulled up. Arnold was trying to make detective. He was one of those arrogant white boys who wanted a name for himself.

"What up Baker, Mr. Grimy himself. I finally get a chance to meet the little kid turned big kid. How's the dope business". Arnold wasn't one to piss off so I kept my attitude in check and just played along with his game.

"If it isn't the notorious and famous blue shirt. Arnold I thought you were bigger in stature. The stories on the street about you make you look like you were a gladiator." We both laughed but I knew his laughter was more sarcastic than mine.

"I'm sorry to hear about Fame. I never want to see any kids murdered. What you say Baker; you think it's time for you to give it up? Life is too short." He said with a grin. I just returned his grin with a grin of my own. He was crafty with his approach.

"Give up what? College? No thanks, education is key my friend." I was starting to ruffle his feathers. His white skin began showing his frustration in the form of red blood filling his face.

"It's only a matter of time before I get you Baker. You know that... right?"

"Get me for what Arnold? Get me for being on this corner. Last time I checked that wasn't a crime. You got the wrong Baker homie. Someone has been filling your head with lies."

I was a fool to think as big as we were no one knew about our activity. It was only a matter of time until the Feds would come knocking. I just didn't think local law enforcement would know who we were. When living a lifestyle like ours only a fool would think it would last forever. It was really time to throw in the towel.

"Well I guess you're going to play this game huh Baker? You pick the wrong opponent this time. We're on to you! You, Sammy, Swampman, Clarkboy, Tony and Hawk! It's only a matter of time before I come for you all. When that time comes I'll be giving you gift in the form of a bracelet and a jersey number but not like that iced out bracelet you have on now nor that Mitchell and Ness covering your back."

He drove off with no smile on his face. I knew it was definitely time to get out. I had plenty of money stashed so money wasn't going to be a thing. I only had to convince the Noize makers of the severe nature of our choices.

An emergency meeting was called to let everyone know what was going on.

"I called this meeting to let you all know the cops are on to us and if they are on to us, best believe the Feds are too. I don't know how and how long but we need to get out now!" Everyone looked surprised. I don't know why. We were drug dealers and that lifestyle wasn't suppose to last forever even though we carried on like it would.

"Why should we stop now? We have enough people. We don't have to touch anything ourselves, let them do it." Tony said with a tone unwilling to relinquish his grip off the lifestyle we were accustomed to. Sammy joined in the debate with the same ideology. Swampman was the only one who saw it as I did.

"I did five years in that box my NGHAS, and I can't do it again, I love all of you but not enough to go through that experience again, I'm with Baker." The room was lopsided. Swampman and I knew it would fall. Our whole entire empire would become rubbish and we would be at the bottom unable to breathe. Money was changing our dynamic. It was a time when a Noize Maker felt a certain way about something the rest would trust his judgment. There was no debate. We understood if it was good for one it was good for all. Time had now changed all that. One side of the room was fighting to continue the operation and the other side was trying to end it.

How do you think Cutta and Panama going to take us dropping out like this?" Tony said with an aggravation fresh on his tongue like morning mouthwash. Hawk joined in,

"We not video game hustling anymore Baker! We too dam big to turn back and just let go. We are pulling in six-figure money a month. Who is going to let that just resign? This isn't Wall Street homie. We ain't leaving with a 401k and a pension. It's either death or jail. We chose this." Hawk was right but we had to try. I would rather fend for my life on the streets then to live it in a box.

"I understand where you all are coming from. We let this happen to ourselves, but it comes a time when enough is enough. This is the time. I got a son now to raise and I can't raise him from inside an 8x7 box! I'm out! You all can divide my share, but I'm done!" I started walking out the room and Swampman followed. Sammy gave chase as the rest of the room's anger pounced me in my back.

"Bake! Wait a minute primo. You can't do this to me!

I looked at Sammy and then gave him a hug.

"I have to Sammy. If you love me the same way I love you, you'll do the same." I walked off with him standing there just watching. The crew that I had grown up with through trials and experiences both good and bad was now about to become no more. We had hurt too many people. We never thought about the lives we were destroying with our greed. Little kids were having horrible holidays because their parents needed what we had. They would sell their valuables and sometime themselves for a fix. Mothers were attending funerals and burying their sons because of what we saw as just business. I wanted no part of it any longer. Life wasn't mine to take. It wasn't even mine to give! I was a murderer, and a selfish money addicted fool!

I didn't know where to turn. Arnold wouldn't fish if he thought he didn't have any good bait to reel us in. He was going to be a problem but killing a cop was out of the question.

Sammy felt like I was abandoning him and the crew.

"We hot Sammy! This life can't last primo! What we gone have matching walkers pushing bricks to people in the retirement home? Not me! I want more!" My words pierced his side like an arrow in the heel of Achilles. He was silent. He sat on the couch and just put his head down with his hands on top of his head, fingers interlocked showing his frustration as he blew out a sigh of tiring patience.

"Why did we let Big Sippi pull us into this life Baker? We were fine selling video games and having fun with our friends. Look at us now. The money changed us!" His pain was felt as each word traveled into my eardrum. We were far into the depths of Hades. We were too deep to be saved so it was no reason to call on Jesus he wasn't coming. We had been judged!

Sammy was right. Big Sippi placed us in the hands of hate and dressed her up in a hooker dress. He paid her and had us thinking all the attention she was showing us was genuine love. We found out it was just business the way she hugged us. She never loved us!

Arnold was seriously on our trail. He wasn't the type to back off once he had you in his sights. I was stuck with an easy but hard choice. I could leave the streets and duck Arnold or I could leave the streets and take the backlash that could come from our departure. We were making too much money for anyone to let us go without an encore.

Arnold's presence didn't stop me from hanging on 35th street. I didn't want him to know I knew he had us. I had to play the game like I wasn't shook by his threats. He would often circle the block and just smile. Sometimes he would stop and we would have a conversation until his sarcastic under tones ended it with a rebuttal that angered him.

"It's only a matter of time until you are talking to me through fiber glass Bake! Then we will see if you are really a killer like they say!"

Arnold was starting to get on my bad side. It angered me that I couldn't do anything to him. Killing a cop wasn't a rule you break but it was a rule that had me thinking.

Money still flowed with Sammy at the helm alone. I would call him from time to time. He really didn't want to talk to me but he loved me too much to ignore me.

"What's good Bake? You need something? I'm real busy right now homie can I link up with you later?"

"I just wanted to see what you were up to and how things were going."

"All is good primo! Let me get back with you. I love you." He was gone quicker than the conversation could begin. I couldn't bare him treating me that way. I knew he needed me but I just wanted to get out before it all went sour.

With me out of the game I had more time to spend with my family. My son was walking and I thought it was no time better than that moment to patch things up with Daja and just put my life in perspective. Things were going great for a while. Daja and I were like we were when we first met and I actually loved it. I didn't cheat on her during those good times and we had a bond that was unbreakable.

Little Bake loved animals so we took him to Norfolk Zoo. We were having a ball and then it happen. I saw Arnold with his family and without tack he just grilled me in front of his and mine.

"Hey, Heyyyy! It's Norfolk's biggest moneymaker. Look kids, this is the drug dealer I was telling you about."

His son asked him if I was the one he was going to arrest soon. He shook his head in an up and down motion. I was pissed!

"My daddy said you and your friends are really bad. You don't look bad, are you? I answered with compassion for his children even though he had none for my son.

"Your Father is just doing his job but sometimes when you're caught up in work you make bad choices and you listen to the wrong people."

I looked at him in his eyes and repeated, "Really bad choices!" Arnold knew what I meant by that. He knew this time he had messed up.

"I'll see you around officer, you have a beautiful family. You make sure you take care of them and Oh, thanks for the disrespect in front of mine."

"Is that a threat Bake?"

"Me...threaten a public servant? Come on Arnold you got me labeled wrong. Only psychos would do that!" I then gave him a smirk from the depths of Hades. He was shook. It was time to find out all I could about him. I wanted to know where he lived and where his kids went to school. I wanted to know what time his daughter went to ballet practice and who took her. I wanted to know what time the dog went outside to piss and which leg he raised. He was totally out of pocket with that move. It was the reason Daja and I started spinning out of control. She flipped out!

"In front of our kid Baker! Your lifestyle is wicked for a family." She was screaming on me in the middle of the Zoo as Arnold looked over his shoulder giggling.

I wanted to snatch the hair out of her head. I just walked away. I took little Bake to get ice cream and left her yelling like she lost her mind.

"Your lifestyle killed us Baker! Your lifestyle has officially killed our family without a bullet!" Arnold had more reason to stay on our trail. Daja put a dagger in me with her tantrum. Little Bake was too young to understand but he felt the hatred because as he ate his ice cream he just looked at me and started crying. I picked him up and felt like the worst father on earth. I never knew I would have kids. I never wanted to have any especially living the life I was living but turning back truly was not an option. My life was over.

he life I wanted for Daja and I was now down! I had no words for her but she was too vindictive to shun her away. I knew how to handle every situation in the streets but this one I had no clue. If I was in it alone I would have just took off and left her with a stack of cash, but I didn't want to be one of those fathers. I just dealt with her from a far and gave her whatever she asked for.

It all went wrong with us when she started keeping my son away from me. I would call and they wouldn't answer. I went to the house and no one answered the door. While in the mall I saw her grandfather. I walked up to him and before I could say anything he told me Daja and her sister moved. I was furious!

"Hello Baker. I know you have questions about your son but I can't help you with them. Daja and Baker are better off away from you. You know how much I love you myself. I just can't accept your lifestyle, and I need you to understand that decision." I just stared. I was crushed. He was right but I wanted my son near me. I asked him if he could at least have them call me to let me know they are ok. He refused and walked away.

With all of my money and power nothing helped with finding my son. I used all the influences I had but their whereabouts stayed a mystery. It was frustrating because I had the ability to find people where they didn't want to be found. It was a skill I learned from Cutta but with the location of my son it was worthless.

Sammy finally gave me a call to see how I was doing. I really missed him but something in his voice wasn't right.

"Hey Primo. I'm calling to ask if you wanted to link up."

Cool Sammy! Just let me know the time and date."

"Remember our spot?"

"Of course!"

"Be there soon as the gun fires off!"

"I got you! See you soon as the whistle blows!"

Sammy was in trouble. We made up code phrases to let each other know when it was about to pop off and what to do.

I told the Noize makers what was up and we all got locked and loaded. Our spot was a little warehouse on 25th street. We used it as a staging point for shipments and it was also our house of horrors. We had it sound proof, so no one would here the screams from the top floor.

I arrived at sundown and once I stepped inside I saw a person whom I forgot about. It was Immortal. He was standing with a gun to Sammy's head.

"I've been looking for y'all Little NGHAS for a long time! It's pay up time my dudes. Take out your heat and drop it. I know you scrapped so don't play me." I took out both of my guns and dropped them on the ground.

"Man! What are you talking about pay up time? We don't have any beef with you?"

"I know it was you who killed my cousin and no it's your turn. Let's see how much you like losing a family member."

"Immortal you didn't care about Fame like we did. We were more family to him than you. I know what you did to your grandfather!"

"Well you got me on that. I never did like the little NGHA. I guess this is about the dough, so where it at?" Immortal clicked back his 44 bulldog and pressed more firmly against Sammy's head.

"I got you homie! Calm down and follow me." Sammy was very composed. I knew he wanted me to make a move and the rest of the crew was already positioned in the warehouse ready to do damage.

"You know what Bake? Forget the money because I'd rather have your life. He pushed Sammy and fired two shots in his back and then came charging at me. I had another guns stuck in my back and when the shots were fired I pulled out with a fury inside and charged back. When the smoke cleared Sammy and Immortal was lying on the ground with blood everywhere. Everyone ran out of their locations and rushed to us. Both were still breathing. I ran to Sammy and Swampman kicked Immortals gun away from his hand.

"What you want to do Baker? I'm ready to hydro shock this NGHA!"

"Wait a minute! He ain't telling us something because it's always about the money." I looked down at Sammy and he was leaking but the bullets appeared to go in and out in.

"Who put you up to this homie?" I yelled as I was getting Sammy up to get him to the hospital.

"You know who hate you little NGHA!" He gargled blood and started laughing. Swampman shot him in both knees and he still wouldn't give up the info. Tony said he was going to stay and make him talk and the rest of us rushed out.

We took Sammy to Norfolk General and but the time we got him in the emergency room doors he had passed out. I was hysterical.

"We need some help now!" Two nurses rushed over and attended Sammy. One of them had a look on her face like it wasn't good. They told us to back up while more helped came. They hurried him into the OR and all I could do was flashed back to easier days. I flashed back to days far away from this life. We made the worst choice and now it was looking dim. I called aunt Marisa but I got no answer. I then called Grand.

"Grandma! Sammy has been shot!" Grand screamed!

"No! Dear God not again. Baker where are you?"

"We're at Norfolk General."

"Did you call Marisa?"

"I did but no one answered."
It's not looking good this time Grand. I'm scared."
"It's in the hands of the most high now Baker. You just calm down. I'm on my way." Things went from bad to worst. I got a call from Hush and he said he had Daja and little Baker. He told me Cutta was going to kill them so he is taking them to Miami. I couldn't find where they were so how in the hell did Hush know? Life was messy for me at that time and I had nothing to clean it up with.

Baker Grimes
Hamza Atoi
CHAPTER FIFTEEN

I needed to occupy my mind while Sammy was in surgery. My thoughts were all over the place. I was a train wreck about to happen. Hush called me and told me he was on his way back to Virginia after he dropped Daja and Little Baker off. He said he was going to leave them with Grimmo and my cousin in Miami. Cutta wasn't going to be able to touch him with Grimmo in the picture so I felt relieved in that department. All I knew was I wanted Cutta dead and all who was in his circle. I had to find a way to keep myself together so I told Grand I had to go. She knew I was all to pieces so she let me go my way. I was no help to Sammy in that current state.

I called Tony but he didn't answer. I wanted to know what he got from Immortal. I called every hour on the hour and by the morning I still had no answer. I decided to call Aunt Marisa back also and got nothing. I was starting to worry. I decided to go to Park Place and see if she was at the spot. When I got there I knew my worst fears were answered. I looked on the front of the stoop and saw "SUFFERATION" painted on the door. It was Cutta's greeting card. He was in Norfolk! I knew once I got inside I would see what I didn't want to see. Aunt Marisa was going to be dead. I pulled out my two 45 caliber Rugers and walked slowly through the apartment.

When I got to Aunt Marisa's bedroom it was a gruesome scene. I don't even want to talk about it. I ran out and fell down on the concrete. I was throwing up non-stop. Sammy was holding on to life in the hospital. Aunt Marisa was dead and Tony was nowhere to be found. I couldn't think straight. I called 911. I set out in the front numb like a tooth in a dentist office. Destiny was now playing games with me. The first one to show up on the scene was Arnold and his partner.

"So what's up Mr. Park Place? I can't believe you called us. What you need homie?"

"I don't have time for you today Arnold just go inside and call the coroner and get my Aunt out of here. They both went inside and came back out as quickly as they ran in. He was gagging and asked me if I saw her.

"Why in the hell do you think I called you? You know I don't mess with y'all cats like that!"

He tried to show a more sensitive side but I was far away from reconciliation after his antics at the zoo. He offered to take me home but I wanted no parts of his comfort.

Just stay the hell away from me Arnold! I'm pretty sure when you have something tangible on me we'll see each other. I doubt that of course!"

"Baker I wouldn't wish this on anyone. You need our help. Someone is sending a message. BAKER! BAKER!" I kept walking without answering any of their questions. He was right however, somebody

198 | P a g e

was trying to send a message and that somebody was Cutta.

I knew Cutta was somewhere close by. He loved to see the face of his victim's family. I called Swampman and Neevak to armor up because it was time for war. I had about twenty soldiers on standby ready to put in work. I had to be discreet in case Cutta and his men were watching. They were waiting for the appropriate time to strike. The first thing I had to do was ride all night so I could find out who it was tagging me. It had to be one of his top henchmen because he knew not to send anybody ordinary.

Neevak came up with an idea. I wasn't with it at first but it made sense. He said I should go to New York and rip shop. Cutta was definitely in Norfolk so it was the prime opportunity to strike out at the things he loved.

I called Uncle Flip and let him know what was going on. He set me up with a crew and an arsenal. Neevak and I caught a flight right after he made the suggestion. We hopped a moonlight plane to LaGuardia. When we touched down uncle flip was there to pick us up with all we needed to get started. I didn't wait at all. The first place we hit was Cutta's restaurant. We killed all of his workers and burned it down. The next spot was one he thought I didn't know of. He slipped up one time and let me know he had a son in Long Island. He was the type who ran his mouth too much when he drank. I never said anything about it because I wanted to hold it in my pocket if I needed it one day. It was one day!

I sent two of the guys Uncle Flip set me up with to do the chore. I told them to keep the son alive but kill everything else around him. If nothing was around him worth sending a message, he was going to have to be the message! I had no time for feelings. Cutta was out to destroy me and the only way to fight was to hit harder. Not only did I reap havoc on his businesses, I also killed his link to his connect. He thought I didn't know about Fruity either but I did my research on Cutta for years. I had him figured out before he even knew he was really going to kill us.

It wasn't time to call home because I didn't want any news on my mind. Neevak and I were on an all out assault. We had only a few hours left to get back to Virginia so we could lock the Fort down at home. It was only a matter of time before Cutta was going to get word about what was happening. Uncle Flip took us back to the airport in the morning and we were back in Virginia by 6am.

Uncle Flip set up a flight for Grandma, Cinda and himself to hit the Dominican Republic. He knew it was too hot to stay in New York. Grand didn't like it one bit but he convinced her it was no other way. I didn't talk to her before she left. I couldn't face her. She knew we was lying the whole time but she didn't know the magnitude. I let her down big time!

Sammy had around the clock security on him because of Arnold. I guess it was his way of saying he was sorry about what was happening to my family. Sammy was now in a coma and life wasn't looking good for him nor Noize. We were all at the hospital when it really hit the fan. Hawk and

Clarkboy had this crazy look on their faces like they wanted to say something but couldn't. Swampman was sitting with his head hanging down and silent.
"Yo! Any one seen Tony?" Everyone remained silent.
"What the hell man! Has anybody seen Tony? I don't want everyone to speak at one time." Clarkboy raised his head up slowly and said he went by the warehouse and nothing was there. There was no body, no blood and all of our work and money was gone.
"What you mean everything was gone?"
"Nothing was there. It was like we never had the building. Somebody wiped us out!" What else was going to happen? We had about thirty bricks and a million dollars in that safe. Only the original six Noize Makers had info on what was in there, so who was the rat?

In a million years you would have never been able to tell me someone in our crew would be a trader. Fame flipped on us but to be honest the original members were all that mattered to me. Tony was the absent member so naturally all suspicions were pointed at him.

I called Hush and he informed me we were definitely at war. He said Cutta hired some killers from Jamaica. They were Kingston's "Top Shotta's." It was time to maneuver and place the troops on the front line. I had been waiting for this from the start. I had an intuition it would all go down like this. Neevak said he had a plan that would draw them into our arena. He wanted to kidnap Panama. I thought he was out of his mind because we didn't need to be at war with two monsters in the game.

"It is do or die time now Baker! We don't know if we are going to make it out but we have to better our chances. If we have to get rid of them both...so be it!" I thought he had gone mad. Panama was cool with me but he was Cutta's number one link. If we took Panama out of the equation it would hurt him drastically but it was also another death warrant. His people wouldn't just sit back and roll over. They would continue to stalk us until we were dead!

I gave Panama a call so I could see were his head was at in all of this. I was trying to gage if Neevak's idea was good.

"What's good P?"

"I didn't think dead men used the phone my friend."

"Who's dead? I'm alive and kicking. You got any news for me funny man?"

"We need to talk in person. Meet me at the strip on 17th street. I'll be on the beach with some pretty ladies." Neevak and I headed out to the boardwalk. Panama had always played the neutral role when it came to any beef in VA, but, now the beef had cross stateliness and I wondered would he still be about money or loyalty. I put in a lot of work for him over the years and got rid of some key people in the process. I wondered if he was going to remember my generosity.

Once we arrived on the strip, like always the cops were everywhere. Greek fest left a sour taste in Virginia Beach officials' mouth. It hadn't been that long since we tore that joint up. I remember being on the top floor of the Four Sails hotel watching Atlantic Avenue burn from the riots. Dark skin was no longer welcome and it was still evident. I never knew why Panama loved to be where he wasn't welcome. He was notorious for walking in country western bars and biker clubs to have a drink. I guess with his monsters with him who was really going to touch him.

The cops watched Neevak and I walk to the beach and followed closely behind. I was strapped so I was a little nervous. Virginia Beach Police officers were known for profiling. I just stayed cool and kept it moving.

I saw P surrounded as he said with three bad chicks. He must have got them off some exotic island. They were flawless.

"What up Baker? Sit down and have some grapes." I sat down and one of the girls began feeding me.

"I appreciate the hospitality P but let's get down to it. Why does Cutta want me dead?" He looked at me and smiled while being fed fresh fruit like a king.

"You blew up too fast kid. He knows you are up next to take over. The powers that be don't like that."

"What powers are you talking about P?"

"I'm speaking of Cutta and his law enforcement buddies. Oh! You didn't know? Cutta is ATF! He has been pushing weight on the side for years. Why you think him so untouchable? He's not the one to rumble with my friend. Cut your losses short and move away. Somewhere no one can find you because this battle you can't win." I was shocked! I knew he was dirty but I never knew he was the law.

"So how you get in it with him? Are you ATF too?

"You're smart Baker. Do I strike you as ATF...DEA...FBI? No my boy, I took a deal long ago that would ensure I would never see the inside of a prison gate. I didn't rat on anyone! No not at all! Cutta struck me a deal before the DEA got to me. He used you all to take the fall I was going to take. The Feds have been on you guys for a while. Either way, you can't win Baker." Neevak was right Panama was worth grabbing but I didn't want to risk it because now I knew they were watching me. I realized how we were played from the start. Big Sippi and Do-Wop's incarceration was just a precursor of what was to be. They let us get big and trained us to be stone cold killers. Cutta gets his big bust and keeps everyone thinking he is just deep undercover.

I thanked Panama for the Information but I could no longer associate myself with him. He was on Cutta's payroll and he played me. When I was doing work for him it really was for Cutta. I wasn't as smart as I thought. The whole entire lifestyle was a set up. Why would he pick us still remained a mystery. I guest destiny was the real organizer. She kept the crew and me within six degrees of separation of all who surrounded us. I couldn't kill Cutta but I had to try if not for me for Sammy! He was still in a coma and things weren't at all good. I talked to Grand and she said he was not going to make it and I needed to leave Virginia. I wanted to but leaving Sammy was out of the question. The only way I was going to leave was when he left, one way or another!

Baker Grimes
Hamza Atoi
CHAPTER SIXTEEN

I was about 19 years old at the time of Sammy's death, and a low-key millionaire. The morning after I received the news he was going to die, I turned into a mad man. It was nothing anyone could do that would've kept me from vengeance. I knew from the beginning, I should have taken care of Cutta and his crew but the money blinded me. He got me! He played me like a fiddle. I was the one who could read even the most well designed lie. All it took was a simple conversation and eye contact in order to get to the truth. How did he do it? Where did I slip up in my pursuit of American pie and what was real? One thing that was true, Cutta was now on the chopping block.

I arrived back in Norfolk International at about 3 am on the morning Sammy died. My Grand called me on my cell and I already knew what was on the other line when I heard the first ring. For the first couple of days I held it together. It wasn't until after his cremation the floodgates opened. I had a room at the Marriott in the presidential suite, and I was sitting in front of the grand piano with a bottle of Remey and an L, then it hit me. I cried for 7 hours straight. Sammy was my life and I now felt lost. After the tears subsided, the evil grew! I was now the most deadly man that anyone would ever encounter because I had nothing to lose. Tony was missing. Hawk, Swampman and Clarkboy were in hiding because of the hit on us. I wasn't going to hide. I felt like come and get me!

Hush was the only one out of all of this that never crossed me. The only thing was this, where was he? I hadn't seen him since everything began. Last I knew of his whereabouts, he had one of Cutta's generals in some warehouse in Queens waiting for me to do what I do. I guess when I didn't show up on time, he thought it was a set up. It wasn't! That wasn't even a thought when it came to Hush. I loved him as if he was my Father!

I called and called but he never answered. This was the only person I ever feared because Hush was just like me. When he loved you he loved you but when he hated you, he hated you. He once told me the only thing he knew how to do was sang and murder and with a face like his, who was going to sign him to a record deal? I wondered if he was upset. One time we had an argument and I said, "He had to be the Feds". All of the things he knew just didn't add up, but the one thing I knew was this, I didn't want a killer like him on the haunt.

Destiny was now starting to turn on me. It was as if destiny was a bitter ex girlfriend who wanted revenge. She wouldn't let up. It wasn't like the old times when I knew she was on my side. It seemed like she wanted me dead because now Daja and her problems entered the picture.

Daja was truly beginning to get on my nerves. With all that was going on, I wasn't able to get around and see my son the way I wanted to. She knew what was at stake, so why would she bug me? I had her in hiding and I didn't even let her family know where she was. She had it all in spite of the bad situation. Its funny how these females ride with you during the good times but fail to realize that you are a drug dealer and killer. That type of life doesn't have a retirement plan, but I guess green is as blinding as looking directly into the sun! If I were blessed to have a baby girl, when she grew up, I would school her about no good guys like me. Yes, we got money and power, but look at where it leads! If I had a baby girl I would tell her go to school, secure her future herself and then pray God sends her a soul mate. With Daja, I knew it would eventually come to what I was about to do. She was going to eventually jeopardize my son's life with all her selfishness

I decided to hop a flight to Haiti where I had her hidden. She was protected daily. She was in a place that no one would've been able to touch her but me! Once I got to Porte-au-Prince. I linked up with my man Grimmo. He and one of his top goons "Pierre" met me and we took a helicopter to Cap Haitian. Once there, I saw that Daja was way out of hand. She was living the greatest living conditions imaginable and had no worries when it came to money or anything else of value. Daja's problem was she loved to floss and in Haiti, with all the kidnappings happening; she couldn't.

There was no one there besides the men protecting her who knew she was loaded. She had no one to see her Gucci slippers or three thousand dollar Louis bag.

She hated that! She wanted to be seen and she didn't care that there was a price on all of our heads. I had her and my son set up in a mansion that I bought from Grimmo. It was on the hillside overlooking the water. From the view there was no way to tell Haiti was a very poor country. The island with all of its poverty was beautiful. I knew as long as I dished out pounds of money and work; I had nothing to worry about inside Grimmo's camp. Once I arrived, Daja was sitting on the terrace drinking a glass of Kremas. She had the look of a mad woman. You would think she would take advantage of a beautiful countryside. I sat down beside her and she had the audacity to say "If Fame was living, I wouldn't be in this predicament!"

I flipped out. I ran off the terrace and went straight to her room and began gathering all of her things. I took her jewels, clothes, purses, shoes and everything she loved. I got Grimmo's men to help me throw it in the pool. My son went out with Pierre to enjoy the countryside so I didn't feel bad about it! She was the most ungrateful chick I had ever met. It was time for her to go!

Grimmo heard all of the commotion and sped upstairs to see what the fuss was about. He took one look at the pool and instead of laughing; he looked in my eyes like he understood the problem. He pulled me to the side said,

"You know we have ways on the island that can do more damage than death!"

That was exactly what I needed. I wanted her to suffer because I really didn't have it in my heart to kill her because of my son. He called to some of his men and we tied her up, gagged her and threw her in the trunk. We rode into this small township that scared the hell out of me. It looked like death. I mean that literally!

As we continued to drive, Grimmo looked at me and said

"What you are about to witness I can't explain just ask no questions and do as I say."

He didn't have to say anything more. Grimmo told me to follow him into this alleyway as the men followed with Daja tide up on their shoulders.

Once we reached our destination, it wasn't what it appeared to be. I thought I was going to smell a foul stench and see heads hanging but no, instead it was a beautifully hidden home that would remind you of a New Orleans plantation home. This huge dude with a scar around his neck escorted us inside. It looked like someone tried to hang him once. When we walked in, I witnessed the most beautiful women I had ever seen. She looked like she was in her early fifties but later found out she was around 85 years old. She was laced in all white from head to toe like a Muslim woman would dress. Her name was Manman Papiyon (Mother Butterfly). She was rumored to be the daughter of the devil himself so of course no one would cross her in any way. She had a sweet eerie feel about her. Although I felt comfortable around her, my grandmother taught me to never drop my guard around those who studied the arts.

Manman Papiyon called Grimmo forward and with his head looking at his feet he went to her side as she whispered to him in Creole. She then smiled and looked at me. Till this day I don't know what she said to him. He came back over to me and asked if I really wanted to proceed with what was about to happen. I looked in her eyes and nodded yes. He then told me that once it is done there is no turning back. At that point I didn't care what happen to her. She then called him back over and summoned me also. Manman once again began to speak in Creole with no one offering to translate. She then reached behind her rocking chair and pulled out an old jar with beads around them and handed me a pair of red and black beads that also had shells on them. Once I placed them around my neck, Manman Papiyon motioned for me to come to her. As I approached she made another motion that I should kneel. Once on my knees, she leaned over from her old creaking rocking chair and kissed me on my forehead. Grimmo looked at me and smiled.

I was puzzled. What was done? What had I agreed to? We all left with one less person on the ride back. When we got far away from the town, I asked Grimmo if all was Ok. He just looked at me with a face of solace and said,

"Pa gen pwoblem"! I happen to look at his neck and hanging under his platinum links, were a pair of red and black beads just like mine. I felt like I had just signed a deal with the devil. Well one good thing that came out of it. I didn't have to worry about Daja's nonsense ever again, and now that she was out of the way, I could focus on the war ahead.

Instead of going back to Virginia, I put my emotions to the side and thought about things for a second. How would I move if I were on the hit? It was time to slow down and stay out of the cross hairs that Cutta had on me. I left my son in Haiti with Grimmo because I knew that was the safest place for him. Grimmo was always there around him growing up and was like an uncle to him.

I decided to go to Miami and lay low. I made a call to my homie *Duke*, and he set up a place for me to crash. The whole entire week I was there I didn't touch the front door. For me playtime was over. It was time to put a plan together so I could kill Cutta because that was the only way I was going to stop this war.

All of a sudden it hit me! What did Cutta love the most on this earth? It was money! The way to get to Cutta was to start ripping away his dough. I had to act fast and pull him out of hiding.

I made a call to an old friend who was a female version of me. Her name was Piggy, my ace on the low. No one knew we were really like that so it was easy for her to move in silence.

She was in New York at the time so it definitely made things easy. I rang her phone once and hung up then repeated the same thing. That was our little code to let each other know who it was. She did the same and left the code on my call backlog to a phone booth down on Jamaica Ave.

"What up Piggy?"

"Hey baby where you been? The streets are buzzing about you and Sammy is it all good?"

I let her know that Cutta was influencing the streets and Sammy was dead! She instantly felt my pain. Piggy was really my soul mate but I just couldn't see us living a normal life even though she was ready to settle down and leave this entire killing thing behind us.

"What you need for me to do Grimy because you know I got you!"

"I need you to gather your girls and start hunting! I want every spot that Cutta owns burned down! Any money you take you, keep and I'll pay you five hundred thousand on top of it!"

Piggy was so in love with me, she didn't even want the money and was willing to give me the money she was going to take from Cutta. I loved her too, but I had to let her know once she was in, and every one found out, it would be a price on her head also. She didn't care, if I asked her to do it, it was whatever! While in Miami, I got the word from Duke that Cutta had been robbed at every major spot he had in New York. Piggy had a load of no loving amazons who were trained to go. She simultaneously sent them out to hit key spots.

It was time to set the traps. I told Piggy to catch a flight to Miami International and we would drive back to New York together. She never made it! I don't know where she slipped up but on her way to the airport she was shot 10 times and left for dead! In my heart I knew I killed her! Cutta was way too advanced for her crew, but I didn't think he would find out that fast. Now it was double trouble! I had to rush and make calls to D.R. for my Grand to leave

La Vega and go to Haiti with Grimmo and my son. I knew she didn't want to but there was no other choice.

My thoughts were racing. What was I going to do? Sammy was dead, Hush was nowhere to be found and the Noize Makers were separated by fear. I was alone. I had no one to depend on but myself. I couldn't call Panama because it was too risky. Cutta knew how close we were. I needed Hush. He was the only one who could help me out of the mess I was in. Without him I was a dead man walking!

I knew I couldn't go back to Norfolk because the heat with the cops was way too heavy. I had always killed for a reason, but the murders I did in Park Place after Sammy's death was out of pure anger. I remember Hush telling me killing was never personal, but for me it was!

I continued to make moves from Miami, but knew that I had to go soon before I was seen. I told Duke to meet at his spot and I would drop some cash off on him for his troubles. He never answered! Duke always answered his phone because that was the type of businessman he was. I don't care if it was 3 am; he said a missed call was missed money! I knew something was wrong! Duke and I were too close for him to cross me so I knew deep in my heart it wasn't that. Somebody had to be around him who was looking for my whereabouts. That would be the only reason in my mind why he didn't answer. Instead of hitting his spot, I left a case of money under his bed and high tailed it out of Miami.

Cutta was still on the move, so it was time for me to make mine.

Baker Grimes
Hamza Atoi
CHAPTER SEVENTEEN

I left Miami like a dope head super charged on powder. I wasn't too concerned about Duke because I knew he could handle his own, he was one of those old Dade County hustlers who turned dope money into hope money!

I had nowhere in particular to go. I knew it wasn't time to go to New York. I also had a feeling the Feds were on me. I knew how they moved and with all of the recent murders in Norfolk, I knew it put up red flags. I had ducked them once, but this time, if they were really on my trail, I was in serious trouble!

My motto in life was this,

"If you thought it was... it is!"

Once out of Florida I thought about it. If I run now I would be running forever, so I said forget it! It was time to pay Cutta a visit! I drove to New York only stopping for gas and to use the restroom. I didn't even eat. I was ready for war.

Once I got in New York, I went to one of my run down spots that no one ever knew about but me.

I was told by Uncle Flip to always have a place no one knows about in case a rat peaks his head out of a hole. I kept an arsenal there for times like this. I grabbed my duffle bag and filled it with enough explosives and guns to burn down the entire Smithsonian. I still needed some help. This wasn't one of those wars where you could do it alone. If I went by myself it was going to be a suicide mission. I needed to hire some independent contractors. I needed someone whose only alliance was money. At the same time it made the situation a little complicated because they could easily turn on me, so in actuality I needed someone who loved both; hated Cutta and wanted to get paid!

Destiny began to change her mind about me. Duke called and told me that Hush was looking for me. He said Hush knew when I didn't come something was wrong so he left to look for me. Duke also said Hush was laying low because he knew Cutta was going to be relentless. He was right because Cutta had begun to touch everything that moved wrong in New York. Hush said he needed to get with me. He had a crew already with him, so all we had to do was take the war to Cutta's front door. It was on! The rage I had in me not only wanted Cutta dead, but also I wanted his pain to last like Sammy's did. I called Hush and told him to meet me in a few so we could figure out how we were going to do it. He told me he would meet me in about five minutes.

"What the FCK you mean you five minutes away, you don't even know where I am," I said with hostility because how in the hell did he know this spot? Then it dawned on me. Hush would never in a million years let anything happen to me. It was times when I thought I saw a shadow in the distance as I entered my spot. I now know it was him. I not only had an arsenal there, I also had 3 million in cash stashed throughout the warehouse. When he got to my joint, I sent down the elevator so he and his boys could come up. I got the shock of my life! I couldn't believe it. Alongside Hush were Hawk Swampman and Clarkboy.

Tony was still missing but I was hyped to see all that was there. It was going to be like old times. We all looked at each other with tears in our eyes and in unison chanted...NOIZE!!! The murder game was set now! There wasn't anyone I trusted more than my crew and Hush. Swampman came over with a bottle of Remey in his hand. He said Sammy brought it for him for when we he got out. Funny how those years flew pass. It seemed like yesterday we were selling arcade time to our friends in Park Place.

"After it's all done Grimy, we gone drink this bottle and get drunk in Sammy and Aunt Marisa's memory!"

I was with it, but to me nothing would ever change what happened to Sammy. I was ready to get it over with, but something on the inside felt wrong. It just didn't feel right. I wanted him dead but it was all coming together perfect. I hated perfection because that was the first sign of trouble. How did Hush find the Noize makers? How did Hush Know where Cutta was? Someone was foul and I could smell the Feds all over it. My next move I had to make with extreme caution. If I had made any wrong movement that showed my hand, I was dead!

"Aye Yo Hush!" I said with sarcasm in my voice.

"I'm glad you on my team because you always know how to find a NGHA!"

He gave me the look I needed. Before he could even flinch, I pulled out my 357 Desert eagle. Everyone looked at me with fear in their eyes.

"Now tell me, which one of you un-loyal and ungrateful NGHAS with him?" I said with intense hatred in my voice.

They continued to look at me shocked! I knew someone in the room had turned federal informant but whom? I couldn't pin point one person.

"It was too easy throughout all of these years for you to know the things you knew. It just took me to now to figure it out!"

Hush looked at me and smiled. He started clapping his hands.

"I knew you would figure it out one day Bake, but I didn't think it would take you so long!"

"So why Hush?" I said with nervousness.

"It was never about you or the Noize makers. It was always about Cutta. It just so happen that you and Noize got pulled in and I didn't expect you all to get as big as you did! You're in deeper than you would ever imagine!"

I was crushed! I knew it from the jump but I didn't want to believe it.

"So what now?" I said with more intensity and a tighter grip on my heat!

"It's over, we got more than enough evidence on Cutta and his connect, all we need you to do is back down and let me handle the rest."

"What happens to us?"

"You turn in all the information you have on Cutta and testify and we can strike a deal with minimum jail time."

Hush was talking stupid! I knew how deep the rabbit hole flowed. If he thought I was going to give up what I knew he was retarded!

"What the hell you take me for Hush? You know if we turn C.I. we are all dead by the end of the month regardless. I like my chances with war!"

Hushed looked at me like the Hush I knew and said, "I can't let that happen, Grimy!"

I looked at Hawk and told hawk to shoot that piece of crap homie. Hawk didn't budge!

"So, are you with this NGHA Hawk? Are going to betray Noize for this NGHA?" I belted with the anger of Zeus!

"It ain't that Bake, It's over, we can't win!"

I was disappointed because Hawk should have known me better. He knew when I did things like that I was fishing. It was a shame he took the bait!

"Dang Hawk, after all we been through homie, why would you do this?"

He just looked at me and lowered his head!

"Hold up Bake!" Swampman said with sincerity.

"We all took the deal Bake! So if you kill Hawk, you have to kill us all!"

I was in disbelief! My mind was racing at a thousand miles per hour. How could they have done this to me! After the hurt set in my heart the anger followed. In my eyes they were all the reason Sammy was now dead.

"So I guess it's like that?" I asked with a smirk on my face. Hush knew what was coming next.

"Don't do it Grimy, we can fix things! It doesn't have to go down like this!"

In my mind that was the only way it was going down. I raised my heat and bust off two shots. One hit Hush in the chest and the other hit him in his head. I looked at the rest of the crew and asked who was with me?

"What do you mean Bake, the Feds are going to be here any minute now!" Hawk pleaded!

"We can't win, ain't nothing we do going' to bring Sammy back!"

He was sadly mistaken! Revenge always has and always has been just that... revenge! It was about get back! I wanted redemption, and the ones I once loved were in my way!

The Noize Makers was never a crew in my eyes because of what they had done. My rage made me fire my next shot at hawk. The bullet pierced his brain with reckless abandonment. My second shot ripped through Swampman's chest like predator. It was only Clarkboy left. He wasn't moved by all that had happen because he knew me the best out of everyone and knew it was nothing he could say to me that would insure his life! He looked at me and smiled.

"It was a good run won't it Bake?

I looked at him with tears in my eyes and said,

"Yeah... it was!" and then I fired my final shot that ended what the feds and Cutta couldn't.

I took all the money my duffle bag could hold. There was no way I was going to get to Cutta realistically, but I felt like destiny had one more favor for me.

Life began to flash in my face and what I had just done couldn't be rewound. As I was about drive off destiny dealt me another blow. The Feds tactical team was all around me. I couldn't win so I just sat on the ground and let them have me. I knew they would beat the mess out of me because I killed one of their own. As they advanced on me, I just balled up and took all of the punishment they could deal because I knew with all the knowledge I had about Cutta and his connect, they couldn't kill me.

Look at what this life did to me! I'm locked up and all my friends are dead or missing.

So, you ask what I'm going to do now. Well, by the time your F.E.D.S. Magazine subscribers read this only God knows, but one thing that's sure, Cutta gone' pay, but don't quote me in your magazine on that my friend.

Message from the writer:

The creation of Baker Grimes…
A character forged from the fire of the inner-city.

Baker is a character that was birth out of necessity. He is a reality I've seen each day in the inner-cities of America. Little boys who were born fatherless, left to be raised by single mothers or no mothers at all often fall victim to a system that incarcerates more than it educates. The apparent need to be more than what poverty offers excites and ignites most youth to take chances. The drug world is the perfect fit "to be or not to be." The risk is known but the celebrity and the detachment from a life of famine is worth it from their view. The worst thing you could have in low-income areas is a name with no meaning. You ask, what do I mean by this? Little boys all over America fight to be recognized by their peers. It may not seem this way but subliminally the message is loud and clear. Fashion has framed a Polaroid of what success looks like, so if you don't have the latest, most expensive garments and shoes, you are looked at as average or sub-par. As parents and village care takers we must ensure our children are provided with opportunities, not America's definition but our own. "Each one, teach one" is a motto that has been forgotten. We need our own systems to fight this systematic machine that creates poverty for their own personal gain. Welfare helps them just as much as it helps, yet conforming us into mediocrity. The regular work force has become a joke to the young black youth. In their eyes, a nine to five has too many hours and those hours don't equal the pay deserved. The youth that are willing to work for a living, legitimately, obtain jobs in burger joints and eventually peer-pressure sets in forcing them into the normal life most black youths commit to.

Baker was a child that found poverty confusing and by no means was he going to ever taste it. the effects of poverty left him determined in all the wrong ways to dodge famine. Even when he wanted better for his life, the lifestyle he knew took control and left him fighting from the bottom to stay on the top.

Education is the key to abolish the very nature of drug hustling. My aunt would always tell me, *"If you knew better, you'd do better."* This statement is so true. We must teach our youth how to do better or Baker will be the nightmare we all must continue to deal with.